Strength

Omega Queen Series, Volume 5

W.J. May

Published by Dark Shadow Publishing, 2020.

This is a work of fiction. Similarities to real people, places, or events are entirely coincidental.

STRENGTH

First edition. July 15, 2020.

Copyright © 2020 W.J. May.

Written by W.J. May.

Also by W.J. May

Bit-Lit Series
Lost Vampire
Cost of Blood
Price of Death

Blood Red Series
Courage Runs Red
The Night Watch
Marked by Courage
Forever Night
The Other Side of Fear
Blood Red Box Set Books #1-5

Daughters of Darkness: Victoria's Journey
Victoria
Huntress
Coveted (A Vampire & Paranormal Romance)
Twisted
Daughter of Darkness - Victoria - Box Set

Great Temptation Series
The Devil's Footsteps
Heaven's Command
Mortals Surrender

Hidden Secrets Saga
Seventh Mark - Part 1
Seventh Mark - Part 2
Marked By Destiny
Compelled
Fate's Intervention
Chosen Three
The Hidden Secrets Saga: The Complete Series

Kerrigan Chronicles
Stopping Time
A Passage of Time
Ticking Clock
Secrets in Time
Time in the City
Ultimate Future

Mending Magic Series
Lost Souls
Illusion of Power
Challenging the Dark

Castle of Power
Limits of Magic
Protectors of Light

Omega Queen Series
Discipline
Bravery
Courage
Conquer
Strength
Validation

Paranormal Huntress Series
Never Look Back
Coven Master
Alpha's Permission
Blood Bonding
Oracle of Nightmares
Shadows in the Night
Paranormal Huntress BOX SET

Prophecy Series
Only the Beginning
White Winter
Secrets of Destiny

Royal Factions
The Price For Peace
The Cost for Surviving

The Chronicles of Kerrigan
Rae of Hope
Dark Nebula
House of Cards
Royal Tea
Under Fire
End in Sight
Hidden Darkness
Twisted Together
Mark of Fate
Strength & Power
Last One Standing
Rae of Light
The Chronicles of Kerrigan Box Set Books # 1 - 6

The Chronicles of Kerrigan: Gabriel
Living in the Past
Present For Today
Staring at the Future

The Chronicles of Kerrigan Prequel
Christmas Before the Magic

Question the Darkness
Into the Darkness
Fight the Darkness
Alone in the Darkness
Lost in Darkness
The Chronicles of Kerrigan Prequel Series Books #1-3

The Chronicles of Kerrigan Sequel
A Matter of Time
Time Piece
Second Chance
Glitch in Time
Our Time
Precious Time

The Hidden Secrets Saga
Seventh Mark (part 1 & 2)

The Kerrigan Kids
School of Potential
Myths & Magic
Kith & Kin
Playing With Power
Line of Ancestry
Descent of Hope

The Queen's Alpha Series
Eternal
Everlasting
Unceasing
Evermore
Forever
Boundless
Prophecy
Protected
Foretelling
Revelation
Betrayal
Resolved
The Queen's Alpha Box Set

The Senseless Series
Radium Halos - Part 1
Radium Halos - Part 2
Nonsense
Perception
The Senseless - Box Set Books #1-4

Standalone
Shadow of Doubt (Part 1 & 2)
Five Shades of Fantasy
Zwarte Nevel
Shadow of Doubt - Part 1
Shadow of Doubt - Part 2

Four and a Half Shades of Fantasy
Dream Fighter
What Creeps in the Night
Forest of the Forbidden
Arcane Forest: A Fantasy Anthology
The First Fantasy Box Set

Watch for more at www.wjmaybooks.com.

Copyright 2020 by W.J. May

THIS E-BOOK OR PRINT is licensed for your personal enjoyment only. This e-book/paperback may not be re-sold or given away to other people. If you would like to share this book with another person, please purchase an additional copy for each recipient. If you're reading this book and did not purchase it, or it was not purchased for your use only, then please return to Smashwords.com and purchase your own copy. Thank you for respecting the hard work of the author.

All rights reserved. No part of this publication may be reproduced, stored in or introduced into a retrieval system, or transmitted, in any form, or by any means (electronic, mechanical, photocopying, recording, or otherwise) without the prior written permission of both the copyright owner and the above publisher of this book.

This is a work of fiction. Names, characters, places, brands, media, and incidents are either the product of the author's imagination or are used fictitiously. Any resemblance to actual person, living or dead, events, or locales is entirely coincidental. The author acknowledges the trademarked status and trademark owners of various products referenced in this work of fiction, which have been used without permission. The publication/use of these trademarks is not authorized, associated with, or sponsored by the trademark owners.

All rights reserved.
Copyright 2020 by W.J. May
Strength, Book 5 of the Omega Queen Series
Cover design by: Book Cover by Design

No part of this book may be used or reproduced in any manner whatsoever without written permission, except in the case of brief quotations embodied in articles and reviews.

Have You Read the C.o.K Series?

The Chronicles of Kerrigan
Book I - *Rae of Hope* is FREE!

BOOK TRAILER:
http://www.youtube.com/watch?v=gILAwXxx8MU

How hard do you have to shake the family tree to find the truth about the past?

Fifteen year-old Rae Kerrigan never really knew her family's history. Her mother and father died when she was young and it is only when she accepts a scholarship to the prestigious Guilder Boarding School in England that a mysterious family secret is revealed.

Will the sins of the father be the sins of the daughter?

As Rae struggles with new friends, a new school and a star-struck forbidden love, she must also face the ultimate challenge: receive a tattoo on her sixteenth birthday with specific powers that may bind her to an unspeakable darkness. It's up to Rae to undo the dark evil in her family's past and have a ray of hope for her future.

Find W.J. May

Website:
https://www.wjmaybooks.com
Facebook:
https://www.facebook.com/pages/Author-WJ-May-FAN-PAGE/141170442608149
Newsletter:
SIGN UP FOR W.J. May's Newsletter to find out about new releases, updates, cover reveals and even freebies!
http://eepurl.com/97aYf

Strength Blurb:

USA Today Bestselling author, W.J. May, continues the highly anticipated bestselling YA/NA series about love, betrayal, magic and fantasy.
Be prepared to fight... it's the only option.

Time is running out...

As an insidious darkness sweeps across the land, Evie and her friends find themselves in a race to fulfill the prophecy. They acquire a ship and make haste for the Dunes. But, as usual, fate has other plans...

Instead of arriving at their destination, the friends find themselves stranded on the shores of a distant land. A land where the rules don't matter and nothing is as it seems. In the quest to band together, powers are tested and relationships are strained. No matter how hard they try to move forward, it always seems like they're falling several steps behind.

A change is coming, but can the friends rise to meet the challenge? Will they find the stone and stop the darkness in time?

Or do Evie's dreams tell a fateful warning... that they're already too late?

Be careful who you trust. Even the devil was once an angel.

The Queen's Alpha Series

Eternal
Everlasting
Unceasing
Evermore
Forever
Boundless
Prophecy
Protected
Foretelling
Revelation
Betrayal
Resolved

The Omega Queen Series

Discipline
Bravery
Courage
Conquer
Strength
Validation
Approval
Blessing
Balance
Grievance
Enchanted
Gratified

Chapter 1

There are a few things one might think when encountering a Carpathian horde...

I wish I'd put my affairs in order.
I wonder how many arrows are in my quiver.
I should have taken the long way around.

A thought that would never cross a person's mind?

I'd really love to rob these guys.

Evie and the others crept out of the woods and into the Carpathian encampment.

As far as infiltration went, it was the easiest incursion ever. There were no gates, no guards, no perimeter sweeps. Most of the dwellings didn't even have doors. Entering the settlement was literally as simple as stepping off one road and stepping onto the next.

Probably because no one in their right mind would be stupid enough to come here by choice.

"Come on," Ellanden urged quietly, "keep moving."

The friends stayed close together, keeping their heads down and sticking to the shadows.

It hadn't been their choice to come either. Their initial hope had been to bypass the settlement altogether and make their way straight to the docks. But while the Carpathians might be rather lax in terms of security, they weren't foolish. They'd scattered their ships along stretches of beach within the camp itself. Short of approaching by water and climbing in from the sea—a tactical nightmare—anyone who hoped to gain entry would have to get there on foot.

It was a level of proximity no one was comfortable with and, as if that wasn't bad enough, the lateness of the hour didn't seem to have any effect on the encampment whatsoever. If anything, more and more people kept pouring onto the streets the further the six friends ventured inside.

"Incoming!"

The princess glanced up just a body plummeted to the ground in front of her, spraying the hem of her cloak with ribbons of greenish-grey blood. It was impossible to know what kind of creature it had been. All that remained were a few dented tentacles, oozing slowly into the dirt.

Eight tiny shoes landed on top.

Seven hells.

The friends lifted their heads in unison, but the window above them was dark—nothing but a tattered curtain blowing in the breeze. Not that it would have mattered. As soon as the beast fell, a chorus of dark laughter echoed from a tavern across the street. The princess cast a swift glance, only to see it wasn't just the patrons doing the laughing. A table of what looked like off-duty soldiers, armed to the teeth, reveled in the grisly homicide just like everyone else.

So much for the rule of law...

"Don't stop—we don't want to be standing here."

This time, it was Seth who ushered them along. His bright eyes flashed to the table of men as well before he ducked his head and kept walking, an oddly blank expression on his face.

Evie glanced once more at the eight-legged corpse before hurrying after him.

Just keep your head down, she told herself. *Just keep walking.*

Strangely enough, it wasn't the murder that had unsettled her as much as the soldiers. They were a far different breed than the ones they'd fought in the forest. Not just in size and stature; it was something about the way they held themselves. Like they wouldn't hold themselves back.

Those Carpathians hunted animals.

These ones hunted men.

Not surprisingly, she wasn't the only one rattled by the scene. The second they rounded the corner Freya quickened her pace, falling into step by Seth's side.

"Did you ever fight a Carpathian?" she whispered. "In the arena?"

There was no need to make the distinction. They were all thinking the same thing.

"Twice."

Without looking away from the street, he lifted a finger to his neck and temple. Even in the shadowy moonlight, Evie could see the silver imprint of a faded scar. She stifled a shudder. Scars didn't come easy to a shifter. And she'd recently seen exactly what that particular shifter could do.

"There's no one watching the village," he continued quietly, glancing back at the rest of them. "The villagers themselves are defense enough. But there are soldiers patrolling the dock."

Ellanden and Asher nodded slowly. If they were doubting their plan, they didn't show it. But there was a quickness to their step and a tension to their shoulders that wasn't there a moment ago.

"It'll be fine," the fae said quickly when he felt the eyes of the group. Unseen behind him, a succubus plunged a dagger into a potential suitor before getting shot in the head. "This place isn't much worse than Tarnaq and we survived that, didn't we?"

...barely...

"There might be soldiers patrolling the docks, but the crew is most likely getting drunk in one of these taverns. As long as we can slip aboard, there's every chance we can..." He trailed off, glancing over his shoulder as the vampire came to a sudden stop. "Ash? What's the matter?"

Asher was frozen in the middle of the street, staring up at one of the store fronts with a peculiar expression on his face. The princess followed his gaze, then froze as well when she saw the skeleton dangling from beneath the sign. Her mouth fell open when she saw the fangs.

Holy crap.

There weren't many things that could kill a vampire. Even a young vampire. Even a vampire as young as the one standing by her side. She shot him a sideways glance, then laced her fingers through his. No effect. Not until she gave a sharp squeeze did he snap out of his trance.

"We should, uh...we should keep moving."

The others nodded silently, but their eyes were still glued to the sign. Staring in morbid fascination as the bones started swaying in the breeze.

"Ellanden."

The prince jumped with a guilty flush, then snapped back into action—leading the rest of them deliberately to the other side of the street. In truth, he didn't know what disturbed him more: the skeleton itself, or the fact that it had been inexplicably dangling from the apothecary.

Can't believe they even have an apothecary. If something got infected, you'd think they'd just cut it off.

With as much speed as possible, the six friends continued making their way to the docks. It wasn't easy. As the moon climbed high above them, the entire encampment was coming to life.

At first, the princess had thought the settlement was reserved exclusively for Carpathians. But as they continued making their way down to the water, she saw many other creatures as well.

Not the kind she was looking for. *Not* the kind she wanted to see.

It was like all the dregs of Tarnaq had ended up in one place. The worst-tempered, the most dangerous, all those special little horrors that made one's skin crawl. They spent the days gambling and drinking in the village, then headed back to the settlement for an evening of entertainment.

In the land of the Carpathians, entertainment meant blood. And given how much blood the princess could see around her, it was truly a wonder there were any of them left.

A sudden shout echoed across the road, followed by a chorus of riotous laughter as what had started as a bar fight turned into a full-on slaughter. The instigator was quickly surrounded by a tight-knit circle, all of whom seemed intent upon doing their own bit of damage. Then a giant man stepped into the middle and ended the fight...by ripping the perpetrator in half.

Evie froze where she stood, forgetting for a moment to breathe.

Even a dozen yards away, she could feel the impact as both halves of the man fell to the pavement. The laughter swelled even louder. The crowd screamed out for more—

"Let's keep it moving."

She jumped a mile when a quiet voice spoke in her ear. A second later an arm appeared around her shoulder, gently yet firmly leading her away. She glanced up quickly, expecting to see Asher, and was surprised that it was Seth instead. The shifter had angled his body between her and the carnage, never breaking his stride as they continued walking up the street.

He alone didn't look surprised by what was happening. Instead of gawking at every silent horror, he slid right through the middle—a decidedly grim expression on his face.

"Sorry," she muttered, flushing with embarrassment. "I guess none of this is new to you."

His eyes tightened, but he kept walking. He kept her walking as well.

"Fights like that aren't uncommon for Carpathians," he replied quietly. "Some people say the idea for an arena came from them."

Evie nodded slowly, thinking this over.

She remembered her father telling her once that he'd been introduced to the Carpathian people in a remarkably similar way. It had been an off-handed comment, said without thought and prompted by an ungodly amount of alcohol. When she'd pressed further, he'd quickly shut down—flashing a tight smile and having the governess whisk her off to bed. But she'd always remember those quiet words. And she'd always remember the look on his face when he said them.

"It's hard to believe all of this happened in ten years," she murmured, looking around at the weather-beaten taverns, the thick grooves worn in the road. "Things used to be so different."

Seth nodded briskly, flipping up the hood of his cloak.

"Yeah, well...things change." He glanced bracingly around the street, looking far older than his age. "That's why you're doing this, right? To change them back."

She gave him a nudge. "That's why *we're* doing this."

He glanced down with the hint of a grin. "I keep forgetting I volunteered to join your little suicide mission. Looking back, I have no earthly idea why. Perhaps the food we were eating had spoiled. Perhaps I wasn't right in the head."

Unlikely as it was, she found herself grinning as well.

"And here I thought you were being gallant," she replied casually. "Maybe even showing off a little, though I can't imagine why..."

As if the implication wasn't enough, she glanced over at Cosette—walking on the far side of the group. He followed her gaze, lingering a moment on the wisps of ivory hair escaping her cloak.

"I can't believe she freed me," he said abruptly, almost forgetting to lower his voice. "In my whole life, I've never...I've never met anyone who would do that."

Evie glanced up, surprised he'd be so candid, then continued walking with a secret smile.

The man might be able to tear apart a grimlock with his bare hands, but he'd met his match in the breathtaking fae. Even if he didn't quite know it yet...

"Which way?"

A sharp voice cut in between them as Ellanden turned around to face the others. Behind him, the street they'd been travelling forked in two directions. Of course neither happened to be marked with a sign, and at this point choosing the wrong one might prove fatal.

Seth stood there with the others before realizing the prince was talking to him.

"How would I know? I've never been here."

Ellanden's eyes flashed. "You're supposed to be our guide—"

"And I *guided* you to the settlement," Seth interrupted. "This happens to be a Carpathian stronghold, Your Highness. I've never set foot inside."

The prince glared another moment then turned back around, muttering under his breath. "Should have left you in the arena..."

Seth stared at the back of his head before turning dryly to the princess. "*That* one I find less enchanting."

She fought back a grin. "You'll get no argument from me..."

A few steps away, the boys were locked in a hushed discussion. Their heads bent together as they gestured between the two paths, but in the end Asher pulled back with a sigh.

"Just pick one," he commanded. "They both have equal risks, so just pick."

It wasn't an easy decision.

If they headed north, there was a chance they'd miss the dock entirely and have to backtrack the way they'd come. But to head south was to venture even deeper into the settlement.

Freya stepped up to join them, more to conceal herself from the curious eyes of a warlock than anything else. "The north is uncertain, but we know for sure there's a ship to the south. We should head that way." She glanced back in spite of herself. "And we should hurry."

Evie wrapped her cloak tighter, feeling the eyes of the settlement's denizens as well. The streets were so packed and chaotic they'd been able to travel relatively unnoticed thus far, but there was no telling when that luck might run out. Already, a series of empty carts was lining up at the far end of the street. It wouldn't be long before news spread that the hunting party had been killed in the forest.

"I agree with the witch," she said under her breath, shivering slightly as another cart rolled past. "The sooner we find a ship the better."

Then we never have to think about this terrifying place again.

Without another word, the six friends hurried down the unlit alley—moving as quickly as possible and throwing occasional glances over their backs. They had a close call when a drunken sailor stumbled blindly into Freya. They had another when a demonic merchant saw Ellanden from a doorway and invited him to come inside. Evie thought they were finally through the worst of it, when a voice called out suddenly... echoing through the night.

"Excuse me, sweetheart. Do I know you?"

The gang turned around to see a Carpathian soldier standing in the doorway of a tavern, a bottle of whiskey clutched in his hand. The rest of his companions were still drinking inside, but he'd set his sights on a new recreation and headed slowly towards them, his eyes locked on Cosette.

"I must have seen you before," he continued with a gleaming smile, tossing the remains of the bottle into the street. "I'd never forget such a pretty girl."

Both Ellanden and Evie reached for their bows at the same time, but stopped themselves just as quickly. The man might have been approaching them alone, but about twenty of his friends were waiting just inside. One wrong move and the entire group would pour out onto the street.

And heaven help us if that happens...

Cosette braced against the pavement, staring back with a warning in her eyes. "I'm afraid you're mistaken. Must have been someone else."

He only smiled wider, stalking towards her like some demonic cat.

"With that face?" he chuckled darkly. "Honey, don't sell yourself short."

Ellanden made a compulsive movement, but Asher grabbed him discreetly—calling out instead: "The girl's spoken for and you've had too much to drink. Why don't you sleep it off?"

The soldier paused a moment, then continued walking.

"Don't be greedy, vampire—you have plenty to choose from. And besides," his eyes gleamed with anticipation, "this one and me go way back. I keep telling you, I—"

The next few seconds were a blur.

One moment, the man was crossing the street. The next, he was pressed up against the wall with Seth's hand over his mouth, Seth's dagger in his stomach. There was a muffled cry and the shifter tightened his fingers, easing him slowly to the ground.

"You don't know her."

The man died a second later, splayed out in a pool of blood.

Seven hells.

Evie blinked in amazement.

No sooner had she turned around than it was already over. A flash of his eyes, a flick of his wrist, and one of the famed Carpathian warriors fell to the ground at his feet.

"What did you do?" Asher breathed in amazement, staring a moment before his eyes shot nervously across the street. "We're not supposed to call attention—"

"Help me move him."

Already, Seth was gripping the man's shoulders—holding him halfway out of the bloody puddle. When the vampire remained frozen he made the request again, more urgently this time.

"Asher, pick him up. We can't leave a trail of blood."

There was a split second's pause. Then, much to Evie's surprise, it was Ellanden who stepped forward—grabbing the Carpathian's ankles and lifting him up. Together the two men carried him around the corner, tossing him carelessly behind a barrel of trash.

"What happened to keeping a low profile?" Asher muttered as the fae walked past.

Ellanden shrugged, glancing at Seth over his shoulder.

"Sometimes you need to make a little noise…"

The shifter wiped his hands briskly, then extracted the blade. He was just pushing back to his feet when he turned around to find himself face-to-face with an angry woodland princess.

"You didn't need to do that."

He nodded quickly, avoiding her eyes. "I know—"

She stepped in front of him, straight into his line of sight. "I can take care of myself."

He stared a moment, then nodded again.

"I know." His hands moved slowly between them, wiping the blood off the knife. When it was clean he slipped it back into its sheath, lifting his gaze to hers. "I'd like to help."

Her lips parted, but before she could say anything there was a fresh chorus of laughter from the tavern and the friends took off back down the road.

The rest of the settlement passed in a kind of nightmarish blur, and it wasn't long before the princess could smell water. Instead of listening to the demonic voices behind her, she focused on the distant sound of waves lapping against the shore. By the time they got to the beach, the camp and all its horrors were nothing more than a fading memory.

But of course, the fates had a new set of horrors in store…

"Is that…?" Cosette trailed off, peeking over the sandy bluff. "That can't be—"

"—a full battalion of Carpathian soldiers," Ellanden finished.

Together, the friends turned around to glare at the shifter in their midst. He held their gaze for only a moment before throwing his hands in the air.

"Hey—if anything, this only exonerates my skills as your guide."

"Really?" Asher asked icily. "And how's that?"

There was a guilty pause.

"...I told you they were guarding the docks."

Chapter 2

Fifty yards.

That's all the space there was between the friends and the ship. All the space between the powder keg behind them and escape into the open sea. Just fifty yards and fifty Carpathian soldiers.

It might as well have been a thousand.

"What's the plan?" Asher whispered, crouched down with the others behind the bluff. When no one answered him, he kicked the fae in the legs. "Ellanden—what's the plan?"

The prince sank an inch lower in the sand. "Why must you always ask *me* that question?"

"Because you get offended when I don't!"

Evie threw her hands between them. "Guys, now's not the time—"

"Here's an idea," Ellanden hissed, "why don't *you* come up with the plan. Seeing as it was your idea to steal a ship from the Carpathians in the first place."

"*My idea?!*"

"'Then we'll just have to take one for ourselves,'" the fae quoted, twisting around to glare at him head-on. "Am I remembering it incorrectly?"

"*Seriously—enough!*"

The bickering came to a petulant stop under the princess' raised hands. She let them stew in the silence for a moment before turning practically to the fae.

"Ellanden, what's the plan?"

The vampire snickered wickedly as the prince tossed a handful of sand in her face.

"You two are the worst. I knew I should never have let you start dating."

Evie's eyebrows shot into her hair. "Oh, you *let* that happen, did you?"

Cosette rubbed wearily at her temples, muttering under her breath. "Anytime, guys...anytime."

"What if I tried to set them on fire?" Freya piped up helpfully.

The others tilted their heads, considering, but Cosette's eyes snapped open with a glare.

"Why is that *always* your idea?"

The witch's smile cooled dramatically. "Because it *always* works."

"It won't work here," Seth interrupted quietly. Unlike the others, he had no previous history or entanglements clouding his judgement and getting in the way. "They're too spread out for you to get them all at once, and they're armed with long-range weapons. The second they realized the flames were coming from you, they'd shoot you on sight."

Cosette's lips twitched up in a smirk. "Not exactly a deal-breaker..."

"What about that mist you created earlier?" Evie asked hopefully. "We could use it to sneak down to the water—"

Freya shook her head. "It only really works on one person, and I doubt I could keep it up in this wind. No, I still say we go with the fire. The rest of you could just stand in front of me like human shields."

Not surprisingly, that wasn't met with the best reception.

For the next few minutes, they went back and forth—each one contributing their own crazy idea before getting shot down like the rest. There was no need to lower their voices. Carpathians might have been gifted with some unholy physical advantages, but advanced hearing wasn't one of them. As the ocean breeze swirled around them the friends continued the increasingly hopeless discussion, until all at once Ellanden held up his hand.

His eyes went first to Evie before coming to rest on the vampire by her side.

"I think your girlfriend should take her clothes off."

Asher stared blankly back.

"What? You want *me* to kill you, is that it?" he finally answered. "Feel more comfortable with some friendly fire?"

"No, he's right," Seth said immediately, looking excited for the first time.

"And *you*," Asher silenced him fiercely. "It's way too early for *you* to be making that joke. We don't even know you—"

Ellanden slid in between them, holding up a soothing hand.

"Ash, I'm saying she should shift."

The vampire paused a moment before turning to his girlfriend. She stared between the three of them, lifting her gaze to the battalion of monsters just over their heads.

"You want me to shift?" she repeated incredulously. "Instead of using some long-range weapons like the rest of you, you want me to take on the horde as a glorified dog?"

Ellanden's eyes sparkled with the beginnings of a new plan.

"Trust me."

"I *don't* trust you," the princess muttered under her breath, stomping behind the fae as they made their way through the sand. "You *know* I don't trust you. I tell you all the time."

Ellanden helped her over a piece of driftwood with a gallant smile. "Here's a chance for us to work on that."

She yanked back her hand, flashing a sideways glare. "Here's an idea: how about we just give you to the Carpathians? I'm sure you can distract them long enough for the rest of us to sneak aboard. You've built such a reputation for stamina—"

"Enough of your talking, woman. Now take off your clothes."

The fae's eyes sparkled as he turned around, staring graciously down the shoreline.

Evie considered taking the opportunity to stab him with his own dagger, but relented with a sigh and began to disrobe. The shoes came first, as there was no saving them. Then with a little more force than was probably required, she whipped off her cloak and threw it at the back of his head.

"Hang on to that, will you?"

He reached back to grab it, then held it up in dismay.

"Everly, I can't wear this. It's for a woman. It'll ruin my whole—"

"Would *you* like to spend the next few weeks on the high seas in nothing but a dress?" she demanded. "That's what I thought. Now be careful not to lose it. Otherwise, I'm taking yours."

He rolled it up without further protest, stuffing it behind his quiver.

"I like your confidence." He answered her questioning look with a smile. "Thinking we'll make it to the water." The princess balked, but he waved her on with another smile. "Carry on."

She stared at him a long moment, then started taking off her clothes. "I'm going to regret this..."

He turned back around with a cheerful grin. "That's what they always say."

IT WAS ONE THING TO feign confidence when the friends were around each other, laughing and bickering to lighten the mood. It was quite another when they left the gang behind and ventured out on their own...straight towards the Carpathian horde.

There was a hitch in Evie's step and even Ellanden hesitated as they rounded the corner and saw what lay in store. For a split second, neither of them moved. Then he pulled a twisted coil from his pocket and knelt beside her in the sand.

"Are you ready for this?"

As a wolf, she was unable to answer. But a silent communication passed between the two as they locked eyes. A second later, he looped the salcor around her neck.

"After all these years of waiting," he joked nervously, "you're finally my prisoner."

The princess tensed automatically, waiting for the enchantment to take effect, waiting for some outward sign of her newfound servitude. There was a reason such things were popular with slavers and jailors. Until the terms of her capture were met, there was no escaping its magical hold.

But nothing happened. Either Ellanden wasn't nearly as strong-willed as he thought he was, or the rope itself had yet to be tested. One way or another, she hoped she never had to find out.

"All right," he stood up briskly, wiping the sand from his hands, "same plan as usual. You just stand there and look depressed…leave the rest to me."

She could have smiled. She bit him instead.

Seven hells!

As it turned out, the salcor worked after all. Even a simple rebellion, even a little joke, and she was rearing back with a yelp of pain—magically punished for raising a hand to her master.

Ellanden looked down with a start, then tilted his head curiously. "Are you okay? Was that the rope?"

She glared up at him, too frightened to do anything more.

"Interesting…" he murmured, staring at the loop in his hand. "I might ask Cosette to let me hang on to this thing…"

She glared again, stomping her foot in the sand.

"You're right—not the time." He filed the idea away for later, stepping fearlessly onto the sand. "We have a ship to steal…"

SAY WHAT YOU WANT ABOUT the prince of the Fae—and Evie had said plenty—the man was a born performer.

The second they set foot on the sand, a kind of transformation came over him. Gone was the caution, gone was the poise. The man who replaced them was about two breaths away from being committed. He threw back his head, tossed back his hair, and used his deadly sword as a walking stick—strolling thoughtlessly forward like an eccentric beachcomber walking his dog.

It was just fifty yards to the Carpathians, but the fae was crossing them fast. When they were close enough to be seen, he lifted his hand with a beaming smile.

"Hello, there! So good to see a friendly face—it feels like I've been walking for ages!"

Wherever he was hiding, Evie could almost feel the vampire cringe. The Carpathians turned around slowly. In all likelihood, they had never been called 'friendly' in their lives.

The one in front looked the fae up and down, lips parting in surprise.

"You must be lost."

You must be CRAZY is more like it.

Ellanden flashed another smile, deciding to be a little of both.

"I'm afraid so." He came to a stop just a few yards away, towing Evie by his side. "Is this the dock that's closest to Tarnaq? I have a ship just around the corner that I'm looking to moor."

When the fae had shared his plan with the others, they thought he was crazy. But truth be told, it was rather predictable in terms of how his plans tended to go.

The fae wanted a ship?

In typical Ellanden fashion, he simply pretended he already had one.

The Carpathian followed his gaze before staring back incredulously.

"You have a ship you're looking to moor?"

If it wasn't so terrifying, it might have almost been funny. The usual menace and aggression had given way to complete and utter disbelief.

"This is a port, is it not?" Ellanden asked charmingly. "Or have I come by mistake?"

Evie's eyes darted between them, waiting with bated breath. By now, some of the shock was wearing off and the soldiers were beginning to realize what a golden opportunity had wandered into their midst. There were several covert glances before another man stepped forward with a smile.

"Not at all. In fact, you should stay a while." He looked the prince up and down slowly, eyes lingering on certain parts. "We'll make sure you have a good time."

Ellanden tensed involuntarily, but never broke character.

"That sounds...memorable." He made a conscious effort not to reach for his bow and kept babbling on with a grin. "But right now all I'm in the market for...*is* a market!"

He laughed loudly, as if he'd made a joke. The Carpathians stared back blankly.

"Let me explain." He took a step closer, dragging Evie beside him in the sand. "I'm in what you might call the hospitality business—providing goods and services to men such as yourselves."

He gave the rope a sharp tug, yanking Evie forward.

Only then did they notice she was a shifter. Only then did they notice it was a magic rope.

"You're a slaver?" the Carpathian asked in surprise.

Ellanden shuddered theatrically, making a show of examining his nails.

"That's such a harsh word. I prefer the term 'facilitator'. People tell me what they're in the market for and I provide it—for the right price."

Seven hells...he actually winked.

The Carpathians didn't quite know what to make of this. There was a series of murmurs from the ones in back, while the other glanced down the shoreline.

"This ship of yours," he said slowly, "it's full of—"

"Merchandise," Ellanden finished brightly, seemingly oblivious to the hazardous consequence of his words. "We've got shifters, nymphs, naiads, witches—you name it. The one things we *don't* have is satyrs," he added seriously. "We had some trouble a few years back."

Evie closed her eyes.

If we survive this, we're staging an intervention.

This proclamation was met with even more surprise. The Carpathians were an invasive people—hunters and aggressors. They were used to tracking down victims, provoking the fight themselves. When prey wandered so willingly into their midst? They were at a bit of a loss.

That being said, they were also a suspicious people.

And the fae was acting more suspicious than most.

"A whole ship full of merchandise, huh?"

A deep voice rumbled from the center of the horde, sending a host of chills racing down Evie's spine. She watched breathlessly as a new man came forth. This one had a bronze notch on his belt, and the others stepped aside with instinctual deference as he slowly made his way to the front.

In hindsight, Evie had to credit Ellanden with standing his ground. If it was possible, this man was even bigger and more frightening than the ones they'd seen before. He wasn't shy either.

He crossed the space between them, standing a full head above the young prince.

"Fae aren't known for being slavers," he continued slowly, fixing Ellanden with a piercing gaze. "As I recall, your kind fought fiercely *against* that sort of thing in the Great War."

Despite all his instincts to scream and run, Ellanden flashed a carefree smile.

"What can I say—times have changed. Now we have to seize opportunity where we can."

In hindsight, he may have regretted using those exact words. The commander smiled, baring every single one of his teeth as the rest of the battalion laughed darkly behind him.

Evie shivered involuntarily, unable to stop herself.

She might have been grateful for the added use of claws and fangs, but each of the soldiers looked much more intimidating from such a reduced height. Especially their commander.

Another man pushed to the front of the crowd, wielding a brutish knife.

"Let's just take the fae and be done with it—"

Ellanden grabbed the blade with a cry of delight.

What are you—

"Is that Dekraxi steel?" He yanked it from the man's hand, running the tips of his fingers along the edge. "*Very* nice. But it's nothing compared to Becatti craftsmanship."

The soldier faltered, tilting his head. "You have—"

"In the hold of the ship." In a sudden movement the prince twirled the knife around, pressing the handle into the soldier's hand. "The ship I'm still looking to dock, by the way..."

By now, the Carpathians were beginning to wonder if he was a touch mad. They stood in silence for a moment before one in the back whispered to another.

"Fae are also known for their love of drink."

Is that a thing?

"Tell you what," the commander offered, gesturing to Evie with a smile. "I'll keep this one as a sign of good faith, then send men with you to see the others. If this 'merchandise' is as impressive as you say, then I'm sure you'd be welcome to anchor at port."

Evie cringed back, leaning into Ellanden's leg.

"Absolutely not," the fae said briskly. "I'm running a business, not a charity. Besides, I'm partial to this one myself." He glanced down with a touch of scorn. "Whatever its deficiencies..."

The commander stared back in silence as the man with the blade pushed forward again.

"I don't think you understand." He pressed the tip to the base of Ellanden's throat. "Where I come from, it's unwise to refuse such a generous offer—"

There was a blur of movement, then the man's arm cracked in half.

"I don't think *you* understand," Ellanden said softly, "where I come from, you get only what you pay for." His eyes flickered to those in the back. "I believe the Fae are known for that as well."

It was a turning point. All that could be done now was wait.

While the fae clearly wouldn't win in combat against them, none of the Carpathians was particularly eager to be the collateral involved in taking him down. Besides, they were intrigued. Not only was the man beautiful, but he was clearly a bit unhinged. Borderline psychotic.

And if there really was a ship...

The commander offered his hand with a gleaming smile. "In that case, you have a deal."

Crap—I forgot the signal!

The princess froze in horror as the two men shook, trying to gather her senses and remember what they'd discussed. It wasn't a fireball, it wasn't a shout—

"Excellent."

Ellanden withdrew his hand as soon as was possible, the smile still lingering on his face. For a split second, time stood still. Then he looked down at the princess, staring deep into her eyes.

"I release you from service."

...*that's it.*

And just like that...all hell broke loose.

Chapter 3

It was hard to say how it actually got started. Everything seemed to happen at once.

As the rope broke free, Evie launched herself into the air—jaws closing around the throat of the nearest Carpathian. At the same time another wolf sprang out of nowhere, attacking the soldiers from behind. At the same time a wave of fire and a volley of arrows came from two different directions, catching the battalion in the crosshairs. And at the same time the commander threw his fist into the air...sounding the order to attack.

It would be the last command he would ever give.

In a decision that probably saved his life, Ellanden didn't reach for his bow. He reached for the salcor instead—lassoing the commander around the neck. The man let out a feral roar and lunged towards him, but was immediately thrown onto his back by the punishing enchantment.

"KILL THEM—"

He tried to shout, but the magical cord tightened once again. By now, the fae had reached for his bow. He nocked an arrow to the string, levelling it at the man's face.

"And you..." he said in a voice too cold and angry to sound anything like his own, "I release you as well."

The rope sprang free just as the arrow flew across the sand, embedding itself deep in the commander's throat. There was one more attempt to yell, one more dizzied attempt to pull it loose and charge forward, then the man went still—never to move again.

Atta boy.

Evie streaked back to his side, arriving just as he threw the salcor again—circling it around the necks of three others. The thing wasn't meant to be a weapon, but it certainly played the part. The moment the soldiers raised their hands against him, they were beaten back with a supernatural power that far exceeded their own. The prince actually laughed aloud, delighted with the spell.

"No need for swords at all. They just need to make this in a bigger size."

She rolled her eyes, vaulting forward to finish the men before they could lift to their feet. But that was the last bit of levity the friends would see. The Carpathians had recovered from the surprise of the attack and were regrouping themselves. At last, all that destructive power had come to a head.

Seven hells!

No sooner had the princess torn into the first soldier than a knife flew out of nowhere, slashing across her side. She let out a cry as Ellanden fired two retaliatory arrows, killing her attacker on the spot, but more were already coming. *Many* more than they could handle themselves.

The friends exchanged a silent look. A wish for luck? A final goodbye? Then they lifted their eyes and braced themselves in the sand...ready for whatever the night had in store.

It was *so* fast.

No matter how many fights and skirmishes Evie had seen since leaving the royal caravan, she didn't know if she'd ever get used to the speed. A flash of silver, the whip of a cloak, the dull impacts as flesh pounded against flesh. It was enough to make one dizzy.

Yet there she was, fighting in the middle of it.

She'd regretted her size earlier, when she'd been looking up at the horde from the ground, but now she saw it as a huge advantage. While the rest of the Carpathians charged around, towering over everything in sight—she darted in between them like a blade. Clawing and biting and inflicting unspeakable amounts of damage. Always gone by the time they'd turned around to see.

On the other side of the battalion, Seth was doing the same thing. Granted, his style seemed a bit more direct than hers…

"Why won't you just die?!"

There was a spray of sand as a Carpathian battle-axe cratered into the ground where the wolf had been standing. It should have sliced him in half, it should have cut straight through the bone, except he was no longer there. The soldier wielding the blade let out a violent curse.

"When this is over, I'm going to skin you alive and wear you as a coat."

This time, Evie was able to see the shifter circling around him. He hadn't escaped the battle unscathed, but his eyes glittered and she could have sworn he was smiling. At the very least, he seemed to take the threat as a personal challenge. Without an iota of fear he threw himself straight on top of the Carpathian, matching blade against fang as the two squared off.

If he hadn't been so distracted, he might have dispatched the man sooner. But the entire time he'd been fighting, the shifter had kept one eye trained on the lovely princess across the sand.

Cosette and Freya had started on different sides of the battalion, but worked their way back together—standing with their backs to the ocean and their feet in the waves. Given their combined firepower, the two had drawn quite a crowd. But so far, they were managing to hold them off.

Granted, there was no telling how long that might last…

"Get down!"

At the sound of Ellanden's voice the princess ducked immediately, dropping to the sand just as two blades crashed together above her head. Her teeth vibrated with the impact but she sprang up regardless, using one soldier to leap onto the other.

It was violent, but it was quick.

She sank her teeth into the one man's shoulder, thrashing about and splintering the bone while Ellanden disarmed his companion. As the spare blade flew into the air, the fae flipped around to catch it. At the same time Evie dove forward, knocking the remaining soldier to the ground.

And then there was none.

Her skin was raw and bleeding. Her whole body ached with unspeakable fatigue. But with a rush of adrenaline, she threw herself onto the fallen soldier.

...and *that* is where her luck ran out.

The moment she leapt forward a bronzed club flew out of nowhere, knocking her straight out of the air. She landed with a yelp of pain in the sand, trying to recover her senses as the giant shadow of a man loomed over her—swinging the weapon back and forth in his hand.

...*ow.*

Never had she felt such a thing. It was as if her entire ribcage had caved inward.

"Evie!"

She tried to twist her head. Ellanden was racing towards her, shouting something that she couldn't understand, but he would never reach her. No sooner had he started running than the fae was overtaken by soldiers of his own. As they swarmed around him, she lifted her eyes once more towards the heavens. The man was still standing over her—still swinging that wretched club.

"It was brave of you and your friends to come here," he murmured, kneeling down so they were eye to eye. Behind him, the spray of florescent fire sweeping across the sand abruptly stopped. The princess shuddered to think what that might mean. "Brave, but foolish. You had to know you were never going to leave this beach alive."

Actually, we were really hoping that wouldn't be the case...

The princess tried to pull in a breath, but let out a quiet whimper instead. Her lungs weren't working. Her legs weren't working. Even her vision was failing—the edges of the bloody picture were beginning to grow dark.

"Asphyxiation," the man said bluntly, squinting down at her in the sand. "Not a bad way to die, but I have something special for you. You see, looking at your friend piqued my interest." He pulled something out of his pocket. "I'd like to see what you look like before you go..."

Before the princess could understand what was happening, the man pressed a common silver coin to the side of her neck. She let out another cry, twisting and writhing, but her strength was failing and the man was using both hands. With a steaming hiss, the forbidden metal burned through her skin—blinding her with pain as it dug its way to the other side. At first, she thought it was a random torture. Not until the air began to shimmer did she understand what he'd meant.

He's going to make me shift back, she thought in horror, imagining herself lying naked there in the sand. *I can't keep up the transformation in this amount of pain—*

Another scream ripped through her as she lashed out with her claws. This attempt was already weaker than the last. It was only a matter of time before those screams became human.

A single tear slipped down her face as she looked desperately for her friends.

It was hard to see anything from the ground, even harder given the violent mayhem spilling over the beach. But she managed to get glimpses. Just glimpses—but things didn't look good.

In just a short amount of time, things had taken a turn for the worse.

Freya was gone. There was no sign of her, save a torn swatch of fabric from the cloak she'd been wearing. On the other side of the battalion, Cosette was out of arrows and fighting with her bare hands. It was a brave attempt, but there was a giant gash on her forehead bleeding freely down the side of her face. As the princess watched she dropped to both knees, blinking in a daze.

Seth appeared to be nursing a broken leg. It was hard to tell in his lupine form, but he was retreating more than attacking and gingerly favoring one side. Sensing weakness, more soldiers were already clamoring towards him—raising their weapons with savage cries.

Which leaves just one.

"EVIE!"

The second she thought his name, the princess heard Ellanden's voice in the crowd. He was fighting his way towards her, massacring anyone foolish enough to get in his way. But in the end, it was just a numbers game. In the end, the friends were simply overwhelmed.

There was a metallic hiss as one of the Carpathians lashed out with a whip-like weapon the princess had never seen before, raking it down the fae's back. A spray of blood flew into the air as Ellanden let out a tortured cry, then the horde closed in and he was completely hidden from view.

The sound of quiet laughter made Evie lift her eyes.

"See—this isn't so bad. Not compared to what it could be." The man holding her prisoner smiled, stroking the silver coin down the side of her face. "And I have to admit, I'm surprised you've been able to hold out so long. Most people would have already...*there* it is."

Like the release of a breath, the wolf vanished and a trembling, naked woman appeared in its place. A trail of blood followed the progress of the coin down her face, and waves of fiery crimson hair fanned out upon the sand. Her eyes tightened with pain as she stared up at the man kneeling over her, but no matter how fiercely she tried to resist she no longer had the strength to fight back.

He nodded slowly, as if he sensed the end was near.

"That's it...just give in." His knee pressed mercilessly upon her collapsed ribs, speeding the process along, then he pulled back with a grin. "Actually, I think we might play a little first—"

A sharp collision threw him onto his back. The coin flew into the air.

The princess blinked in a daze, still lying in the sand, when the silhouette of a man appeared in the sky above her, two glistening fangs shining in the moonlight.

Asher.

His body curved slightly as the Carpathian pushed to his feet, hovering over her like a guardian angel—one who may have spent some time on the dark side in his misbegotten youth. A quiet hiss escaped his lips, and suddenly the princess realized what was so strange about his posture.

He wasn't just protective. He was territorial.

"You?"

For a split second, the Carpathian simply stared.

It must have been a strange sight—a shifter and a vampire. Historically, the two peoples didn't get along. Historically, vampires didn't get along with anybody.

But Asher was in no mood for talking. A single thought occupied his mind.

With a speed and savagery that left her truly breathless he threw himself upon the soldier, forgoing conventional weapons entirely and ripping the man apart with his bare hands. There were screams and snarls. Sudden splashes of blood painted the sand. For good measure, he picked up the silver coin—holding it aloft before pressing it straight *through* the man's face.

Needless to say, he died...badly.

Asher stared down at him for a moment before turning to the naked girl in the sand.

"Love?"

She let out a kind of gasp, then rolled suddenly to her side—coughing violently as the bones in her chest finally started to repair. The vampire was beside her in a moment, whispering soft words of comfort and steadying her with gentle hands. A monster one moment, an angel the next.

How does he do that? How does he switch between them so well?

The second it was over, he lifted her gracefully to her feet. She leaned against him as he draped his cloak around her shoulders. He smelled of kerosene and pine. When they pulled apart his eyes were shining with concern, but the battle was still raging.

"Will you be all right if I—"

"Go," she interrupted immediately, grasping the hilt of a sword.

The next second he vanished—moving so quickly it was like he was never there.

At this point, it was the only thing that might save them. Vampires were hard enough to track on the best of days. They were damn near impossible if you didn't know they were coming.

Asher swept across the beach like a vengeful tide, destroying anything and everything that crossed his path. Soldiers fell to the sand with shouts of astonishment. Weapons flew into the air as he tore through what remained of the battalion, dark vengeance shining in his eyes.

One by one, he fought his way to the rest of them—dragging Freya from behind the sand dune, ridding Seth of the soldiers fighting against him, ripping apart those men attacking Cosette with such ferocity the princess almost had to hide her eyes.

Just a few seconds, then only one person was left. Granted, he was also in the most trouble.

Ellanden had been fighting with a skill and fury to match even the vampire's, but he'd been doing it much longer and that legendary endurance was about to run out. Almost half the soldiers on the beach had swept towards him at the same time, overwhelming his efforts to fight back.

It had finally proven enough.

Just one mistake—that's all it took. Just one moment of hesitation as that deadening fatigue sank into this arms. Then they leapt upon him like a plague, claiming death before its time.

The first strike knocked him backwards. The second knocked the blade from his hand. The third would have taken his life but, ironically enough, it was his beloved bow that saved him. As a battle-axe swung from behind the curved wood absorbed the blow, shattering on the spot.

He dropped to his knees, no longer able to see the others.

True to form, he didn't call for help. Warriors of the Fae were unspeakably proud, and he'd been raised in the heart of the ivory city. Instead he simply lifted his eyes, watching as the crowd parted and a solitary man came through.

The same man whose arm he'd broken. A man still wielding the same brutish blade.

There was no wind-up or sinister speech. Without ever breaking his stride he strode forward and plunged the knife straight into the fae's chest, lodging it deep in the bone.

Ellanden cried out in agony, lifting his hands to dislodge it. But the Carpathian wrapped his own hands around the handle, refusing to let go.

"Clever boy," he sneered, pushing the blade in farther. "But the thing is, you actually did me a favor. You see, with our commander gone, I'm the one in charge."

Like the rest of his friends, most of the damage the prince sustained had been blunted by adrenaline. Unlikely to fully manifest unless he survived to the next day.

But *this* he felt.

As the blade twisted in deeper he let out a soft cry, bowing his head in pain.

His hands were trembling. His breath was coming in shallow pants. Yet when the man stepped closer to finish the job, he stared straight at him—completely fearless, even in the end.

Evie stumbled forward, eyes wide with fright. She was still clutching the sword, but she was too far away to do anything but watch as one of her two best friends silently met his death.

NO!

The blade tore from the fae's chest in what looked like slow motion. The scream that followed echoed in the night. The Carpathian soldier raised it once more, preparing to end things once and for all. But as it sliced through the air—

—a man appeared in between.

It was hard to tell who looked more incensed, the Carpathian holding the blade or the vampire holding his wrist. Just based on what happened next, Evie would guess the vampire.

Even all the way across the sand, she imagined she could feel the impact. The dull thud as the Carpathian's head detached from his body and buried in the sand. She hadn't even seen Asher do it. The rest of the soldiers were still reaching for their blades. The only one who didn't look particularly fazed was Ellanden. He simply reached for the vampire, half-collapsing against his side.

"What the hell took you so long?"

Asher's lips twitched, though he never took his eyes from the Carpathians. "You know us vampires, so easily distracted..."

At this point, the remaining soldiers seemed to reconsider their options. They took a step back. Then another. Then they glanced around and realized they were the only ones left. The beach was a graveyard, a smoldering wasteland of sand and blood.

The one in front opened his mouth to call for reinforcements. The settlement was close enough that, even cavorting inside the noisy taverns, other battalions might still be able to hear his call. It was a call that would have ended things. But it would never come to pass.

As he pulled in a breath a final wave of fire swept over the length of the beach, incinerating every Carpathian soldier who stood in its path.

STRENGTH

Evie's eyes glowed with the strange light, but it was gone just as quickly as it had come. Leaving nothing but the waning light of a silver moon.

And a blood-soaked witch, kneeling shakily in the water.

"And with that...I retire."

The friends laughed weakly as they slowly came back together, limping across the sand. Not all of them could manage. The second Ellanden tried to stand, he collapsed into the vampire's arms.

"Just take it easy," Asher soothed, lifting him gently. "I've got you."

Instead of firing back with his usual sarcasm, the fae let out an exhausted sigh and closed his eyes—allowing himself to be half-carried across the sand. Not until they were halfway there did he pull back in sudden alarm, staring at the vampire's blood-soaked shirt.

"Asher, wait..." His hands lifted weakly to his chest, trying to stem the bleeding, but there was no point. It was all over both of them. "Are you—"

"I'm fine," Asher replied calmly. The two stared at each other for a long moment before he offered his arm once more. "I'm in control. I promise."

The rest of the friends were already waiting when the two men finally joined them, assessing their own injuries and trying to evaluate what supplies they had left. The salcor had been lost, but the woodland princess had already recovered it. Most of their weapons had been broken, but there were plenty scattered around the beach. No doubt there were even more waiting on the ship.

Evie lifted her eyes in the darkness, staring out towards the sea.

I can't believe this is really happening...

Somewhere beyond the black expanse of water, the Dunes were waiting. And somewhere within that wretched hellscape, a mythical stone was waiting as well.

Months of travel. Unspeakable sacrifice. Countless miles crossed.

The moment was finally upon them.

"So that's the ship, huh?" Freya asked, more to break the silence than anything else. Her clothes were torn and her arms were bleeding, but her voice was strangely calm.

The others followed her gaze, peering up at the shadowy sails, then Seth cocked his head with a little grin. "Unless you'd like another. I'm sure there's another battalion further up the beach."

Evie stared another moment at the water before turning back to the others. "Last chance to walk away. Once we step onto that ship...there's no turning back."

For any of us.

Her eyes lingered on three people in particular—the three who hadn't originally set out with them on the quest. Rather than avoiding her gaze, they stared back intently.

After a few seconds, Cosette stepped forward.

"I'm coming." Considering she'd lost several pints of blood, the young fae was surprisingly steady. She slipped a dagger into its sheath before nudging the witch. "Freya's coming, too."

That's four...

"I get seasick," Freya blurted. Her cheeks colored as the rest of them turned incredulously, then her eyes flickered to Ellanden. "But yeah, I'm coming, too."

That's five...

"Seth?"

To Evie's surprise, it was Ellanden who asked the question. Perhaps he'd seen the shifter fighting and decided he was a valuable asset. Perhaps he'd simply lost an obscene amount of blood.

The shifter looked up slowly, glancing at the lovely princess by his side. Their eyes met ever so briefly before he gave her a little wink.

"I wouldn't miss it."

That's six.

STRENGTH

It wasn't what she'd envisioned, and it certainly wasn't what she'd been counting on. But maybe, just maybe, it was what the fates had always had in mind.

※

EVIE'S FIRST THOUGHT stepping aboard the ship was how strange it was that the Carpathians hadn't given it a name. The first thing sailors in both her father's and her mother's navy did once completing a vessel was to christen it with a name. Yet the bow of this ship remained blank.

Her next thought was how much bigger it was than it had looked from the shore. There was a reason these kinds of maritime voyages came equipped with a full crew. As she gazed up at the masts, she felt suddenly nervous the six friends wouldn't be able to handle it alone.

Fortunately for them, the crew of this particular ship was indeed getting drunk in the taverns as the fae had predicted. With a battalion of soldiers patrolling each of the docks and the ship itself at anchor, there wasn't reason to leave a single man behind.

At least, that's what they thought upon coming aboard.

"I don't much care what they have in terms of provisions," Freya whispered, hurrying after the others as they made their way to the deck. "As long as there's some kind of bed—"

"If there *is* a bed," Asher interrupted, "Ellanden gets it. And I don't want to hear a word of argument from anyone. He needs to rest."

He had been quietly fretting over the prince since their departure from the beach. Of all the injuries they'd sustained, a stab wound to the chest was by far the most serious. What worried him even more was that the notoriously stubborn fae wasn't even refusing his attempts to help. Aside from a few half-hearted protests, he'd allowed himself to be carried along.

"It's fine," Ellanden mumbled, trying hard to stay awake. His boots shuffled weakly against the slick wood. At times, they didn't even touch the ground. "*I'm* fine, Ash. You can let go."

The vampire's eyes tightened as he adjusted his grip.

"If I let go, you'll fall over," he said softly, glancing for the umpteenth time at the fae's blood-soaked clothes. "I really wish you'd let me take a look. It wouldn't take much time—"

The fae tried to laugh, but ended up coughing instead.

"We did all this to steal a ship, remember?" He grimaced in pain as they made their way up the stairs, lifting a bracing hand to his chest. "It'd be a real shame if we forgot to do that last part."

"Yes, but..."

Asher trailed off suddenly as they stepped onto the deck. At a first glance, the place looked deserted. Not until a closer look were they able to see—

Holy crap!

The friends stopped cold as a Carpathian sailor turned around.

He was even bigger than the soldiers they'd fought on the beach. And there was something familiar about him. It took the princess a moment to place what it was.

"Holy crap!"

This time, she said it out loud—staring in open-mouthed amazement as she recognized the man they'd met in Tarnaq, the one who'd told them the gruesome tale about the fae archer he'd dragged away from battle and trapped in a cave. It was the stuff of which nightmares were made and, needless to say, it had earned a permanent place in her mind. As had the man who'd told it.

He stared back in equal surprise, pushing slowly to his feet.

"You?"

It was phrased as a question. There was simply no explanation for what they might possibly be doing on the ship. He didn't call for anyone. He appeared to be the only person on board.

"Ellanden," the vampire said sharply.

The fae had pulled away from him, stepping forward to bridge the gap between the two groups. If the princess remembered the encounter in Tarnaq, there was no doubt that the prince remembered as well. His eyes dilated ever so slightly as he took a step closer.

"From the bar," he said quietly, reaffirming it to himself. "You were at the bar."

He went suddenly cold.

"Telling stories..."

The Carpathian straightened up slowly, one hand drifting to his blade.

The odds may have been stacked against him, but he'd beaten worse odds before and these teenagers were already bleeding. There was no doubt in his mind that he could do it again.

"You remember my story?" he asked with a smile. The fae was still beautiful, but he looked as though a strong wind might finish him. "You remember what happened in the end?"

His fingers hovered just above the blade, another strapped and waiting on his back. But the prince made no effort to attack; he simply stood there, gazing back at him in the dim light.

"I remember," Ellanden said softly. "I remember everything."

There was a moment when time stood still. Then—

Seven hells!

As the Carpathian drew his blade, Ellanden ripped a sconce off the wall and plunged it deep into the man's side—exactly where he'd boasted of stabbing the captive fae in the woods. A feral roar exploded out of him, but it never made it off the ship. Faster than sight the fae whipped out an arrow and shoved it into his mouth, burying it to the hilt.

"From my friend at Alenforth," he breathed, giving it a vindictive twist. "With his regards."

With that, he ripped out the arrow—taking a good deal of the man's face with it.

Evie and Asher froze in shock. Cosette was grim. Seth looked like he was reassessing a few things. Only Freya took a step closer, peering down with a disapproving frown.

"Must you be so disgusting?"

The fae shot her a look, then collapsed against the vampire.

"Just don't set the ship on fire."

"Come on." Evie stepped quickly over the body, leading the way onto deck. "We've got to get this thing out of the harbor before anyone else realizes what's going on."

There was no real strategy to the way the friends accomplished this. No real finesse. The lines were cut, the gangplank was kicked aside, the anchor was pulled from the water and dumped unceremoniously upon deck. Once that was finished the ones who were able climbed swiftly up the rigging, cutting whatever ropes they could find that were holding the sails back.

It was a small miracle—but it worked.

As the giant sheets unfurled, they took the ocean breeze with them—opening into a gentle curve as the ship started drifting out towards the sea. Direction didn't matter. At this point, all the friends wanted was to slip into the night before anyone on land was the wiser.

There was a moment where they actually thought they'd made it.

Then the heard the shouts.

"Shit!" Evie leaned over the railing to get a better look, squinting into the darkness as her hair whipped around in the wind. "There's two of them!"

Despite the overall speed of their little insurrection, it seemed not every crew member was drinking at the taverns. No sooner had they slipped into the water than a pair of ships appeared behind them, closing in on either side. Even so far away Evie would see the silhouettes of sailors racing about on deck, lighting torches and pointing ahead. Each ship boasted a full complement and they wouldn't stay far away for long. They may have just taken to the water, but they were catching up fast.

"Let's get you inside," Asher murmured, still supporting the fae. "You need to rest."

The others turned around incredulously. He alone wasn't gazing out at the water. He alone didn't have a look of terror splashed across his face. Even Ellanden woke up enough to stare at his friend in disbelief, wondering if perhaps he'd suffered some kind of mental trauma on the beach.

"Are you serious—"

"Stop moving your arm," Asher commanded quietly, lowering him onto the deck. "It's a miracle you're still even breathing, so let's not push things farther—"

"*Ash*." Ellanden wrenched himself free, pointing blindly into the night. "What does it matter? There are two Carpathian ships out there—"

"Oh—that?" The vampire glanced over his shoulder before shaking his head. "I already took care of that. Don't worry about it."

...come again?

"Don't *worry* about it?!" Seth stepped in between them, staring at the vampire straight on. "I have no idea what chance you think we have, but unless you've got some sort of—"

Asher rolled his eyes, passing off the prince.

"Take him."

In a fluid motion, he took the bow off Cosette's back and fitted an arrow into the string. A moment later he leapt onto the railing, pointing that arrow straight at the oncoming ships.

The friends stared up in silence, then Freya shook her head.

"Seven hells…he's gone mad."

It looked utterly ridiculous. A single man with a bow against two Carpathian ships. While it may have been a striking image, it was hard not to agree with the witch's assessment.

"Babe," Evie approached him slowly, "I like the confidence, but—"

He pointed the arrow suddenly at Freya's heart. "Light it up."

It took the witch a moment to figure out what he meant. Another moment to unlock her frozen hands long enough to douse the arrow in fire.

Evie took a step backwards, shaking her head.

"Honey, what are you—"

"Just a moment," he murmured, squinting slightly into the wind.

The friends watched as he stood there with perfect balance, the flaming arrow lifted to his chin. Despite the rocking of the ship he was so still that he might have been a statue, keeping his hands perfectly level as he peered silently into the night.

Then, all at once, he let the arrow fly.

Evie let out a gasp as the ship behind them caught fire. The *entire* ship. The flames shot up the mast like they had a mind of their own, engulfing the sails before devouring whatever was left of the deck. It was already beginning to sink when a second flaming arrow flew through the night, burying itself in the hull of the second vessel. It went down just as quickly, vanishing into the murky waves.

"Am I dreaming?" Ellanden murmured, lifting a bracing hand to his chest. "Is this real?"

Considering he'd lost well over half his blood, it was a fair question. But the others didn't know what to tell him. They were still standing silent when the vampire leapt back to the deck.

"You asked what took me so long on the beach?" He glanced at the flaming ships, shrugging with a modest smile. "I figured we might need some insurance for our escape."

Behind him the first vessel split up the middle, capsizing into the sea.

Kerosene, the princess remembered suddenly. *He smelled of kerosene and pine.*

"*That's* where you were?" Cosette asked incredulously. "You were sneaking on to both ships while we were fighting? But you were only gone a few minutes—"

"A few minutes is all it took."

Unlike the others, Asher felt no need to boast in his accomplishments. As the rest of them stared in shock at the flames dancing across the water, he simply turned back to his friend.

"Enough stalling, it's time to rest."

Chapter 4

You'd think it would be impossible to sleep after what the friends had just seen. You'd think their minds would be reeling with nightmares and trauma, that the injuries they'd acquired would sharpen and they'd lie there for hours, trying to breathe through the pain.

But that wasn't the case.

Within seconds of lying down each member of the quest instantly succumbed to fatigue, drifting into a dead slumber the moment they'd stretched out upon the floor. The only thing perhaps indicative of the struggle it took to get there was that they did it together. There were many rooms upon the vessel, crewmen's quarters and a galley alike. But they lay down together on the floor of the captain's cabin, loosely intertwined and dreaming.

The only one who didn't join them was Seth. He alone couldn't be convinced that the danger was behind them, that more of those horrors weren't chasing after them in the night. He bid the others goodnight, then slipped back outside and climbed to the top of the tangled rigging, staring silently out towards the sea. The others would find him there in the morning, fast asleep.

Evie woke up naked. *Not* exactly what she had in mind.

With a quiet gasp, she bolted upright—clutching the edges of Asher's borrowed cloak as her eyes darted around the cabin. She needn't have worried, the others had already left. Even her boyfriend was nowhere to be found, but she suspected from the noises she was hearing on deck that he was attempting to doctor the others. More specifically, a highly-irritable fae.

That's fine, she thought, having fallen victim to the vampire's 'helping' hands many times herself. *Let him stay focused on Ellanden. Things are bad enough as it is...*

Even having discovered her newfound shifter abilities, the princess was expecting some degree of damage the next morning. Perhaps a cut that hadn't quite healed. A fading bruise to remind her what happened on the beach. It soon became clear she'd *massively* underestimated things.

"Son of a harpy!"

She let out howl the second her feet touched the floor—curling them back up immediately and deciding to simply live below deck until further notice. *Some* degree of damage?! It felt like her entire body had been beaten to within an inch of her life and then dragged along the beach.

Probably because that's what happened...

In a bloodshot haze, little pieces of the fight started coming back to her. The slash across her shoulder, the muffled crack in one of her hands. Everything began to blur after the Carpathian with the club had knocked her out of the air, bashing in her lungs in the process.

With a secret whimper she lifted a hand to the base of her ribcage, flinching involuntarily the second she touched the skin. She didn't want to guess what it might look like, but the pain had set in and every breath felt as though she was inhaling glass.

No problem. She gingerly settled back on her makeshift bed. *I just won't breathe then. I won't breathe, and I'll stay down here—*

"Planning to stay down here forever?"

Her eyes shot up to see Asher standing in the doorway. 'Secret' whimper? There was no keeping secrets from a vampire. Especially when his girlfriend was just below deck.

"No," she snapped defensively, flinching again as she tried to shift higher on the blankets. "I was just down here planning. Thinking strategy, tallying supplies...we are on a *mission*, Asher."

The vampire's eyes twinkled, just as they had when they were kids. "You and Ellanden should start a club," he replied, sitting down beside her. "People whose pride is *literally* going to get them killed one day."

"You really think that?" she asked brightly, forgiving him on the spot. "You really think I have more pride than anyone else?"

He snorted sarcastically, propping her up against the wall. "Yeah, crazy. You won that competition as well."

The smile faded when he peeled back the cloak, surveying the damage for the first time. The princess stared back warily, trying to interpret the slightest change of expression. Vampires were notoriously hard to read, but a single glance at his face said it didn't look good.

"I don't think it's that bad," she preempted, as though just saying it might be enough.

He lifted his eyes slowly. "Have you seen it?"

"No, but I...I decided I don't think it's that bad."

He stared a moment, then shook his head with a sigh. "You and Ellanden have that in common, too..."

She gulped nervously, trying and failing to pull in a breath.

Since setting off on their fateful quest, the princess had grown accustomed to many things that might have surprised her. Hiking for twelve hours without rest, no longer noticing if the sky above them had started to rain, actually looking forward to a supper of under-cooked squirrel. The one thing she *couldn't* get used to was the rudimentary medical maintenance. Snapping bones back into place, bandaging wounds...those were the details her fairytales had always tended to leave out.

"You should go check on him," she said hopefully. "He's in a *lot* worse shape than me—"

"I already did check on him," Asher said patiently. "I managed to get almost that entire wound sewn shut before he kicked me down the stairs."

Some might have found this shocking. The princess found it rather sensible.

"Well, you can't just go around playing doctor without people's consent."

His eyes snapped shut with a grimace. "I keep telling you, that doesn't mean what you think—"

"At any rate, I don't consent," she continued haughtily, trying to keep herself upright before giving up and sliding petulantly to the floor. "I'm a *shifter*. I don't need to suffer your feeble attempts to heal me any longer. I have the power to—"

"That's exactly what I was going to say," he interrupted. "All the damage I'm seeing is on the inside. There's nothing I can do. You'll have to shift."

The princess stopped cold, the look of victory frozen on her face.

"Uh…now?" she stalled. "Just…just shift right now?"

He tilted his head, a sarcastic smile playing about his lips. "Unless there's a problem. Unless you don't *want* to for some—"

"No, no, I'll totally do it." She grabbed him, pulling shakily to her feet. "I just need to be up on deck. You know, take advantage of the space. Get a little fresh air."

Avoid shifting entirely because that would be SO bloody painful.
Also, I'm not entirely sure that I can…

"Sure." His eyes twinkled as he offered his arm. "Makes sense."

The two of them made their way out of the tiny cabin and up onto the deck. While the princess knew they had technically been drifting on the water all night, it was still a shock to look out and see nothing but open sea. On the one hand, their troubles with the Carpathians were clearly behind them. That being said, she had no earthly idea what was going to happen next.

"Watch your step," Asher said softly.

She glanced down to see the mangled body of the Carpathian sailor lying where they'd left him at the base of the stairs. In the cold light of day, it was quite easy to see what had killed him. She wondered why anyone hadn't bothered yet to throw his body over the side.

"Lovely," she answered, stepping gingerly over the corpse.

The others were lounging together in the middle of the deck. Perhaps 'lounging' was too casual a word. Recuperating was more like it. At a glance their positions were rather casual, but it was clear they didn't have the strength to make them anything else. The dead Carpathian wasn't the only thing that looked worse in daylight. The friends were wearing that battle right on their skin.

Freya had massive burns lacing up both arms—either from some devilish act of the soldiers or her own fire gone out of control. Cosette was leaning against the captain's wheel, tilting so dizzily it would be a miracle if she could stand.

As well as the princess could remember Seth's leg had been broken, but now it was hard to tell. He alone wasn't sitting on the deck, preferring to lean against the railing. But he was putting absolutely no weight on it, and every time the ship rocked a wince of pain shot across his face.

That just left the fae.

Ellanden had taken advantage of the vampire's absence to arm himself and lifted the blade threateningly as they approached. "Not another step. The world could always use one fewer vampire."

Asher held up his hands innocently, settling beside him with a grin. "Far be it from me to impose. The last thing I'd want is to offend a facilitator such as yourself."

There was a burst of laughter, and even Ellanden bowed his head with a smile.

Of all the things that had happened yesterday, the fae's performance on the beach was perhaps the most unbelievable. It was also the most deranged.

The vampire confiscated the sword, shaking his head. "That came far too naturally to you."

"I told you," Cosette said to Freya, "he's certifiable."

"Nonsense," Seth argued, lifting a worn tankard in salute. "He's outstanding. That was one of the stupidest and bravest things I've ever seen."

Ellanden grinned before he could stop himself, forgetting their eternal feud. A second later, he perked up as the smell of alcohol wafted over the deck. "Is that ale?"

"Whiskey," the shifter answered with a smile. "It seems the Carpathians were kind enough to restock the ship before departing for the taverns."

The fae stared up in amazement, looking like some small part of him had come back to life. "Are you serious?"

"I'll get you a tankard."

THE REST OF THE DAY progressed slowly. None of the friends was exactly at their best, and once they discovered the stash of supplies in the hull of the ship they decided to take a day to recuperate and returned to the main deck, basking in the sun and enjoying their well-earned feast.

"What is this?" Evie asked, sniffing delicately at a piece of jerky.

"I wouldn't eat that if I were you." Seth eased it from her hand with a wink, tossing it back on the pile. "Carpathians don't have the same dietary standards as the rest of us."

Trying awfully hard not to wonder what that meant, she turned to Ellanden instead.

"Speaking of Carpathians..." She raised her glass in salute. "You said we needed to get better? There were fifty Carpathian soldiers on the beach. *Fifty*. And not one of us died."

"That's not true," Ellanden muttered.

The prince had abandoned the picnic and was cradling the pieces of his broken bow like a child. Only Cosette seemed to share his sentiments, sitting close beside him and rubbing his back.

The princess lowered her glass, fighting hard to keep a straight face. "My apologies...I forgot two of you are in mourning."

Both fae missed the sarcasm.

"There's *whiskey*," Freya said incredulously, waving the bottle. "There's *food*. And for once, there's no one trying to *kill* us. You'd think all that would be enough to put a smile on your face."

Ellanden shot her a glare and muttered something in his native tongue. Cosette smirked beside him before returning gravely to the bow.

The witch threw up her hands, but Asher chuckled softly.

"On that note, I should probably see if there's anything for me—"

Seth jerked back reflexively as the vampire pushed to his feet—a compulsive gesture he wasn't able to control. He kept his eyes down and his hands moving, peeling a tangerine like it had never happened. But Asher came to an instant stop, staring down with the hint of a smile.

"Someone's jumpy."

Seth glanced up in surprise. "Me? Not at all."

Ellanden abandoned his lamentations long enough to join in with a cruel laugh. "What did you expect, Ash? He saw you on the beach. I'd be jumpy, too."

Asher's face tightened in mock concern. "You might not have had many dealings with vampires, but when I said I was going to find something to eat...I didn't mean you."

The men laughed again as Seth dropped his gaze with a thoughtful smile. He let them go at it a few seconds before lifting his head and looking each one right in the eyes.

"I've haven't had many dealings with vampires, but I've seen what they can do. Any child of the kingdoms would tell you the same. Those aren't the kinds of images you can ever forget."

The laughter stopped abruptly.

"Now if you're really feeling thirsty, there's a barrel of raw meat in the back of the hull." The shifter's lips twitched up in a vengeful grin. "Perhaps we can find you a straw."

※

THE AFTERNOON PROGRESSED in similar fashion. As the sun made its slow trek across the sky, the friends whiled away the hours on the main deck. Either by the necessity of their injuries or simply the company, none of them was at all inclined to leave. Neither were they inclined to get the ship moving in a more deliberate fashion. As long as the troubles that chased them were temporarily held at bay they were content to take a moment for themselves, reveling in the calm before the storm.

Some were trying to put it from their minds. Others had a slightly different approach.

"...the Dunes."

Evie kept her eyes shut, though her shoulders fell with a little sigh. For the last five minutes, she'd been hearing the words with increasing inflection and regularity. She'd sought comfort with Asher, laying her head across his lap, but it seemed there was no escaping them.

"...the Dunes."

The others never shifted position. Most didn't open their eyes. The only one who even took the time to reply was Ellanden, and he did so with increasing impatience.

"Stop saying it."

Freya ignored him, lying on her back and staring up at the sky.

"No point in avoiding it...*the Dunes*." She rolled suddenly onto her stomach, propping up on her arms. "You know, they say avoiding a word gives it power. You should all be chanting like me."

Asher stifled a sigh, running his fingers absentmindedly through Evie's hair. "And yet we're somehow restraining ourselves..."

The witch ignored that, too, returning to her original position. "I read a book once—a book about *the Dunes*—that said it was full of abnormally-sized creatures. Bugs as big as horses. Beasts that could touch the sky. Do you think that's true?"

"Absolutely not," Ellanden replied curtly, though he refused to meet her eyes. "These days, it's nothing more than a sprawling wasteland of sand. The only danger is mixing fact and fiction."

"It *isn't* fiction," she insisted. "At least, that's not the section where I found it."

"Oh, you found this book at the library?" Seth asked innocently. "The one that you—"

"—that we fell out of, yes." Evie snapped at him with a glare.

While most of their adventure thus far read a bit like a tragedy, the shifter couldn't help but find humor in certain parts of their sordid tale. As if these delightful observations weren't enough, he was always gracious enough to share with the rest of them.

"*...the Dunes.*"

"You know, I still don't know why we brought him along." Ellanden flashed the shifter a chilling look. "We haven't needed help thus far. Even with the horses—"

"The horses?" Seth interrupted cheerfully. "The horses that turned out to be kelpies?"

The fae went quiet, glaring murderously at his drink.

"So my question is this," Freya sat up tipsily, swaying a bit from all the alcohol running through her system. "What does a bug the size of a horse *do* all day? Where does it sleep? For that matter—where do regular-sized bugs sleep?"

Cosette shook her head slowly, staring up at the sky. "This is why I don't let you drink whiskey."

"Are you kidding?" Evie grabbed the bottle, fighting back a wince as a stab of pain shot through her ribs. "The whiskey is the only thing keeping her alive."

STRENGTH

"What was that?" Asher asked accusingly, sitting them both up higher so he could get a better look at her. "You flinched."

"I didn't—"

"You haven't fixed it yet? The only reason we came out here—"

"Oh leave her alone, Asher." Cosette tossed a cork at him, feeling a bit tipsy herself. "The girl has more important things on her mind."

"That's right," Freya said crossly. "We were *talking* about bugs."

"You quarrel like family," Seth murmured with a smile. "It reminds me of—

"—of your uncle?" Ellanden interjected. "The one who sold you as a slave?"

A sudden hush fell over the ship as five pairs of eyes turned his way.

"Oh, come on!" He threw up his hands. "How is that not the same thing?"

The friends settled gradually back into place, avoiding each other's eyes and passing around the bottle. After a while, they opened another. A while after that, Freya mumbled under her breath.

"This will be the least of our problems when we get to *the Dunes*..."

THE HOURS DRAGGED BY as the ship drifted farther out towards the open sea.

For the most part, nothing had changed. The fae were still grieving the demise of their beloved bow. The rest were doing their best not to laugh openly and say something they might regret. It was going just fine until Asher suggested the might hold a memorial service.

That's when the fae decided to forget the quest and throw him overboard.

That's when the rest of them decided to make themselves scarce.

"Just remember your training—you'll be fine." Evie flashed a sweet smile at her boyfriend, waving farewell as he was shoved violently against the railing. "I'll see you later...or not."

She spun around on her heel, heading back towards the captain's cabin, but a hand shot out of nowhere and pulled her out of the doorway—back onto the main deck.

"Seth!" she said in surprise, staring up at the tall shifter. "What's wrong?"

"With me? Nothing." His eyes twinkled as he looked her up and down with a smile. "How about you...couple of cracked ribs?"

She froze instinctively, then yanked her arm back with a defensive flush. "No."

He didn't challenge it. He didn't say a word. He simply stood there, leaning against the railing with a patient smile, until the princess' composure finally cracked.

"Fine—they're completely shattered, all right?" She circled around the corner, out of sight from the others. "I can't breathe. I can't fix it. And I'm probably going to die."

He chuckled quietly, joining her by the sails. "You're a theatrical bunch, I'll give you that."

She started to deny it, but the vampire was being forced by knifepoint off the plank. Instead, she folded her arms stiffly across her chest—biting her lip at the extra pain it caused.

"You just need to shift," he continued. "I don't know why you haven't done it already."

...because it isn't that simple.

"Why haven't *you* done it?" she fired back.

He gestured down at himself. "I *have*. How do you think I'm walking around on this leg?"

She glanced down, noticing for the first time.

Growing up in the Belarian palace, she'd seen firsthand the miraculous power of shifting. A man in her father's guard had once fallen from the top story of the castle, but survived because he'd landed as a wolf. She had no doubt that shifting was the answer to her problems now.

There was just one little problem...

"I can't do it," she muttered.

He tilted his head with a frown. "Sorry?"

"I said that I can't do it," she answered through gritted teeth. "Every breath hurts like hell and I can't concentrate enough to…" Her cheeks flamed and she turned away quickly. "I just can't do it, okay? Let it go."

Most people would have left. Especially most strangers. But Seth was different than the people she was used to. And she was shocked to realize they'd left the title of 'strangers' behind.

"Didn't your father teach you this?"

She lifted her head slowly, pale with rage. "Excuse me?"

"I don't mean to offend," he said quickly, eyes dancing with curiosity. "It's just…you're the daughter of a shifter. The most famous shifter in all the realm. How is it possible you wouldn't—"

"Because I've only shifted a handful of times."

He took an actual step back in surprise.

"…really?"

Her cheeks flushed again, but she was unable to answer. It was one thing confessing it to Freya. It was another to speak of it around those she considered family. But it was something else entirely to discuss such things with another shifter—especially one as naturally gifted as Seth.

"Go on, make your jokes." She tried to smile, but found herself on the verge of tears. "It's not like I don't feel ridiculous enough already—"

"You misunderstand me," he interrupted. "I saw you fighting on the beach. You were able to do something like that…and you've only shifted a handful of times?"

High praise. Especially considering who she was speaking to.

She warmed with a secret smile, tucking her hair behind her ears. "It's nothing compared to you. I've never seen anyone fight the way you did in the arena. It was unbelievable."

He shrugged, surprisingly modest. "It got the job done."

She laughed shortly, used to dealing with egos far greater than his own.

"'It got the job done'?" she quoted sarcastically. "I could never fight like that."

"Of course you could," he said easily. "It just takes practice." He paused a moment before adding, "So does shifting on command."

She let out a painful sigh, staring out towards the ocean. "At last, the point emerges..."

He laughed quietly, stepping into her line of sight.

"Sorry if I'm not willing to let it go, Princess. But in case you haven't been listening to Freya all day, we're heading to *the Dunes*. Call it self-preservation, but I don't want the only other wolf in the party fighting for breath with a pair of broken ribs."

She threw up her hands, flinching once more. "It's not like I haven't been trying! I've been trying since the second we stepped onto the ship."

He nodded patiently, reminding her suddenly of her father. "What happens when you try?"

Her eyes narrowed sarcastically. "I stay human."

"That's terribly clever, Princess." He stared deep into her eyes, never losing that unshakable calm. "Just remember that my bones aren't broken. And I can shift just fine."

She glared up at him in silence, then lowered her gaze in defeat.

"You know that feeling you get right before it happens?" she asked softly. "When everything kind of sharpens?" He nodded intently, still staring into her eyes. "Well, that's where it stops for me. I'll get to that point, but before anything can happen the pain comes back and I can't even breathe."

He grimaced sympathetically, nodding again.

"The pain makes it harder," he admitted. "But the principle is the same. All that's stopping you is a basic fear response. You think it will hurt more to shift, but it won't."

"It will—"

"I *promise* it won't." He raked his hair back, shivering a bit in the evening breeze. "And as far as that feeling goes, you just need a little motivation."

She laughed painfully, lifting a bracing hand to her ribs. "Motivation. I couldn't have better motivation."

He stared down at her for a moment, then without a word of warning he ripped off her cloak—leaving her completely naked aboard the freezing cold ship. She reeled back with a gasp, wrapping her arms across her chest. But he was already walking away—taking the cloak with him.

"Now you do."

Chapter 5

After another dreamless night, the six friends reconvened on deck the next morning. They were anxious and sore, but well-rested and well-fed for the first time in what felt like ages.

They hadn't slept together, but had spread out in various quarters on the same deck. A few had tried exploring, but there wasn't much on a Carpathian ship that would bring a smile to one's face. The whiskey was by far the highlight. When they'd discovered a large holding room full of cages, manacles and chains, they decided collectively to leave and lock it behind them. Seth hadn't said another word for the rest of the evening. Shortly after, they'd turned in for the night.

"Good morning," Asher called brightly, joining the rest of them on deck.

The others waved distractedly, mid-breakfast, while the princess looked down with a smile.

"Morning."

Unlike the others, she and Asher *had* slept together. Granted, sleep was all they managed to do. After being tricked naked and left with few options other than canine transformation, the princess had grown rather attached to the idea of clothes.

"You're not hungry?" he asked quietly, sitting down beside her.

She shook her head, shooting the shifter a vengeful look. "Still suffering the after-effects of hypothermia. I imagine it will be quite some time before I manage to take a bite."

Seth grinned, taking a swig of cider. "Yeah, but I bet you can breathe now, right?"

Deciding not to answer, she pushed to her feet—stepping gingerly through the makeshift picnic and resting her hands on the giant wooden wheel behind them. Growing up, she'd taken many voyages to the coast with her parents, mostly to inspect her mother's navy or christen a new ship. Quickly bored by the logistical drivel, she would flee the adults with her trusty guards, Mace and Hastings, and go off in search of just such a wheel. When she was younger, the guards would take turns lifting her so she could see to the horizon—spinning it violently and shouting warnings to imaginary pirates and sea creatures alike. When she was older, she stood on her own—gazing silently towards the horizon and secretly longing for all the adventures yet to come.

Much the same way she was doing now.

Only this time, she knew what was waiting on the other side.

...the Dunes.

Freya could soften it all she wanted through jokes and repetition, but there was something inherently chilling about the words. It was like the place itself could feel them coming, whispering dark greetings and sending them across the sea.

The princess shivered in the morning breeze, drawing her emerald cloak around her. In three days' time they would reach the sandy shores. Two days if the wind held. Then at last they would see it. Then at last they would get the answers to all those questions that plagued them in the night.

Where is the stone? Who else is after it? Have they reached it already? ...which one of us is going to die?

A dull ache settled into her shoulders, one that had nothing to do with what happened on the beach. Try as she might, it was impossible to forget the opening words of their mantra. They'd burned into the princess' mind from the moment the witch said them in the carnival tent.

Three shall set out, though three shall not return...

Her eyes tightened as they drifted between Asher and Ellanden—laughing obliviously at some forgettable joke. If the fates were right, then one of them wouldn't be going home with the others. Their first adventure was destined to be their last.

Or maybe it's me.

The princess turned away, staring back across the water. Wouldn't she prefer it? That she should be the one sacrificed, so neither of the men she'd loved since childhood would have to die? Her every instinct screamed *yes*, and yet it was impossible to truly wish for one's own demise.

I could make it happen, she thought suddenly, her body going suddenly cold. *In the moment of reckoning, I could take fate into my own hands and make it happen. To satisfy the prophecy. To save their lives—*

"Evie?"

She whipped around with a gasp, smiling quickly when she saw Asher standing there. He looked unspeakably beautiful—bathed in the golden sunrise with the ocean breeze in his hair.

"What were you thinking about?" he asked softly. "Your gaze was a million miles away."

She hesitated a moment, then smiled as best she could.

"You," she answered truthfully.

It might be impossible to lie to a fae, but it was nearly impossible to lie to a vampire as well. At least *this* vampire. He had always been too good at reading people. Ever since they were kids.

"Me," he repeated with a little smile, stepping forward so his arms circled her waist. In the beginning, they'd been too nervous to actually touch each other. Now, they could hardly keep their hands to themselves. "What about me?"

She kissed him before he was ready, pulling away before he had time to react.

"That," she said quickly, averting her gaze. "I wanted to do that."

He froze where he stood, staring back with the hint of a frown. But before he could say anything, the others abandoned what was left of their breakfast and joined them. That horizon was beckoning everyone. They were suddenly anxious for the sails to open and the adventure to begin.

It took them a second to realize everyone else was doing the exact same thing.

"Asher," Ellanden prompted, lowering his voice like the vampire had done something embarrassing, "let's go."

The vampire stared blankly, still holding the princess in his arms. "What do you mean?"

It was silent for a moment, then the fae cocked his head towards the rigging.

"Do the, uh…the sailing thing."

The sailing thing?

"What are you talking about?" Asher said bracingly. "Why would you ask me to—"

"Why wouldn't I ask you to?" the fae interrupted with a hint of alarm. "I thought—"

"Wait a second," Evie cut them off sharply, looking between them. "You're telling me that neither one of you knows how to sail?"

This time, the pause was much longer. Then both men started speaking at the same time.

"Of course I do."

"Since I was a child."

"I was just making sure he did."

"What a stupid question."

A hush fell over the ship.

"Are you KIDDING me?!"

The vampire raised his hands, trying to calm things down.

"Look, Evie—"

"You can't be angry with me," Ellanden said stiffly. "I've been stabbed."

"Let's see if I can!" she shouted. "Let's see if I can find it in me!"

Asher tried again to intervene. "If we could all just calm down—"

"You really thought that *I* would know what to do with this thing?" Ellanden interrupted, glancing up at the towering sails. "The whole time you've known me, you thought I'd been sneaking off and taking sailing lessons on the sly?"

"Taviel is an *island*!" she cried. "I thought you might have *some* idea—"

"Honey, just take a breath—"

"Don't HONEY me!" She whirled around, jabbing a finger at the vampire's chest. "This is your fault more than his anyway!"

It took Asher a second to change course. "Why is it..."

She silenced him with a dangerous look.

"Since you were the one who suggested stealing a ship in the first place, I kind of assumed you'd know what to do if we ever got on-board!"

Sensing an opportunity Ellanden positioned himself behind her, folding his arms across his chest. "I assumed that, too, Asher. We couldn't be more disappointed."

"Oh, give me a break—"

"Would all of you just shut up?" Freya stepped quickly in between them, holding up her hands. "I don't care whose fault it is—we're here now."

The three friends glared petulantly, avoiding each other's eyes.

"So let's just figure this out," the witch continued, trying hard to hide the panic and speak in a rational tone. "You've all been on ships like this before. Where do we start?"

It was quiet a few seconds, then Ellanden gestured up to the mast.

"Well, this rope is clearly important..."

Seth slumped back against the railing, rubbing his eyes. "Seven hells, we're all going to die."

"No, we're not." Cosette pushed past him, heading towards the mast. "We're going to sail."

The others watched in amazement as she flitted up the rigging, flying from rope to rope as if she had wings. Her hands were always busy, knotting something here, cutting something there. One by one the heavy sails unfurled, blowing open as they cupped the ocean breeze.

The current grabbed them. White waves started lapping against the hull. By the time she was finished they were cutting smoothly through the water, heading out towards the open sea.

Seven hells…where did that come from?

"It isn't perfect." She landed gracefully beside them, shooting both of her adopted brothers an exasperated look. "I also assumed the two of you had at least *some* idea what you were doing. But, short of any complications, it should take us in the general direction of the Dunes."

Her confidence faltered when she turned around and saw their baffled expressions.

"I mean…at least we're heading due west."

The men were temporarily speechless, but Evie started to smile.

"Where did you learn to do that?"

"I worked on a fishing trawler for two months before heading to Harenthall." She tightened one of the ropes, squinting against the wind. "This is a little bit different, but I assume the general principles remain. A ship is a ship."

Sure enough, there was a quiet sound above them as three more sails rolled open, filling with the ocean wind. There was another burst of speed as the ship glided evenly across the water.

Three days? I bet we make it by the end of tomorrow night.

"You worked on a fishing trawler." Seth's eyes twinkled as they looked the little princess up and down. "Of course you did."

Ellanden pushed deliberately between them, knocking into the shifter's shoulder as he went.

"You want to help get us there faster? Why don't you whittle yourself an oar?"

THE FRIENDS MIGHT HAVE spent the previous day recuperating, but the next few hours were all about preparation. Together, they scoured the holds of the ship—taking anything they thought might be useful and dragging it up to the main deck. They were indeed lucky that the Carpathians had decided to restock their supplies before heading to the taverns that night. As long as the wind held true, they'd be arriving at the Dunes with more than they could have possibly hoped.

Food and fresh water, basic medical supplies, rope and crude satchels—along with a thick sheet of canvas Ellanden was convinced he could make into a tent. All things considered, it was exactly what they would have packed themselves before heading out on a long quest.

And of course, it wouldn't be a Carpathian vessel without weapons...

"Seven hells...I wouldn't want to be on the receiving end of that."

Evie glanced up as Seth settled beside her with a grin, gesturing to the barbaric club in her hand. Both ends were pointed, with half a dozen serrated blades in between. Though perhaps the most unsettling feature was the massive hook sticking out of the side.

The princess flipped it over, examining the hook. "You think that's blood or rust?"

The shifter glanced at her and decided to lie. "Rust."

She set it down carefully, picking up some arrows instead and sorting them slowly into quivers. He watched her working for a moment, then began to help.

A few minutes passed before she glanced from the corner of her eye.

"...you hiding from the vampire?"

He smiled in spite of himself, holding an arrow in each hand.

"I'm not hiding from the vampire."

"Are you sure?"

"I'm sure."

"There's no shame in it."

STRENGTH

"I'm *sure*."

She nodded innocently, returning to the arrows.

The two sat there in comfortable silence—dividing and counting the arrows, passing the ones the other couldn't reach. It was a rather odd task, even more so given that they'd only known each other a few days. And yet, there was something strangely natural about it.

The princess glanced up at him again, peering from beneath her lashes.

"So you really knew what you were doing back at the settlement," she said quietly, watching his reaction. "The rest of us are lucky you were there."

Now that the shock of the Carpathian encampment had begun to wear off, little details were starting to come back to her. The way the shifter had shaken off the nightmares much faster than the rest of them, walking with his hands in his pockets and his eyes on the street. The way he'd pulled the drunken soldier into an alley, gutting him with a blade before hiding the body in the trash.

He let out a quiet sigh, keeping his eyes on the arrows.

"Those people are all the same. You act surprised, they'll want to surprise you more. You react in any way, they'll find it engaging. The best thing to do is be indifferent, just walk away."

Even if that doesn't always work.

She stared up at him, debating whether to ask her next question.

"...did you learn that in the arena?"

There was a hitch in his breathing. His fingers paused over the arrow.

It was something no one ever talked about, though it was never far away from the shifter's mind. Only a few weeks he'd spent in captivity but they were burned deep inside of him, plaguing him with a thousand blood-stained images he'd rather forget.

"The arena is only about survival," he finally answered. "It's just...it's just impossible to think about anything else."

She nodded slowly, letting the conversation drop.

They continued working for a while—both imagining a world that no longer existed, both silently wondering if it could ever come to be restored. Almost all the arrows had been sheathed and sorted when he turned to her suddenly, flashing an unexpected smile.

"Can I ask you a fantastically ill-timed question?"

She let out a burst of laughter, leaning back on her hands.

"What have you got?"

His eyes drifted across the ship, coming to rest on the two fae. They were standing by the railing, talking in their native tongue, completely oblivious to their silent audience.

"Ellanden's very protective."

Not exactly a question, but he'd asked one all the same.

Evie laughed softly, following his gaze.

"You know their story. You know what they've been through. Ten years he was lost, ten years she tried to find him. Is it any wonder they can't be separated now?"

"No," Seth answered honestly. "No, it's not." But he glanced at them again before returning to the princess—a twinkle of mischief in his eyes. "Ellanden's *very* protective."

She laughed once more, pushing stiffly to her feet. "Let me ask *you* a question: how much do you know about fae?"

He stood up alongside her. "Only what I've read."

She took his arm with a smile, leading him slowly down the stairs. "Let me put it this way...have you ever seen a pack of lions in the wild? And they look really cool from far away, but then you realize you're too close and you start to get scared? And then they circle around behind you and you realize you're in trouble? And then you start dating one of their cousins and the pack decides to rip you to shreds? Just tearing and biting and screaming—"

"Yeah, I got it," Seth laughed, holding up a hand. "Thanks for the warning."

She flashed a grin, tossing back her long hair.

"I'm not trying to discourage you. I'm saying it's going to be tough."

"I can do tough."

"It might even be impossible."

He came to a stop when they got to the base of the stairs—gazing across the deck at the woodland princess. She was stringing a bow with a thoughtful expression, nodding along as she listened to whatever Ellanden had to say. It was a rather serious image for one so young, but every now and then the sun would catch her eyes. Every now and then she'd look up with a smile.

Seth stared for a suspended moment, then turned back with a wink.

"Nothing's impossible..."

The two parted ways, heading for opposite ends of the ship. The shifter left to position himself within conversational distance of the girl he admired, while the princess went out in search of her own paramour. He was reclining on the banister, staring out towards the sea.

"You get that you're, like, a hundred feet up, right?" she called, squinting with a grin into the ocean breeze. "A whole ship at your disposal, but you want to lie down on the very edge."

Asher turned with a gentle smile, opening his arms. "Join me?"

She scrambled up without a second thought, balancing precariously on the narrow banister before he gathered her effortlessly into his arms. A soft kiss pressed to the back of her head as she lay back against him, tracing her fingertips along the backs of his hands.

"The arrows are all sorted. All nineteen million of them."

He glanced down in surprise. "Seriously? I was going to help you with that tonight—I thought it would take ages."

She shrugged, staring out at the churning waves.

"Seth gave me a hand. Just like he did with the shifting last night."

In his own unique way.

She hadn't shared the man's tactics with her boyfriend. Best not to test a vampire.

"I know Landi's not crazy about him," she continued, "but I'm glad he's here. The guy's really easy to talk to. And, to be honest, it's kind of nice to have another..."

She trailed off, not wanting to offend.

"Another shifter?" Asher finished with a hidden smile.

She glanced over her shoulder, measuring his expression.

"Is that weird? It's one thing talking with my dad about stuff like that, but that's part of the problem—he's my *dad*. There's only so far he'd ever actually push me. It's totally different with someone my own age, someone with a completely unbiased perspective."

Someone who isn't afraid to strand you naked on a ship, if that's what it takes.

"It isn't weird at all," Asher said softly, tightening his arms. "There were a few younger vampires in some of the camps my father and I visited. It wasn't exactly..." His body tensed before relaxing with a quiet sigh. "Well, I guess it wasn't exactly the same thing."

Evie sucked in a breath, but said nothing.

Considering how much of the vampire's life had been spent travelling the five kingdoms with his father, trying to rally the scattered factions of his kind, they spent surprisingly little time talking about it. That was probably because Asher made a concerted effort not to spend time thinking about it. Whatever memories he did have, he tended to keep to himself.

"And it isn't surprising about Seth," he continued suddenly. "There are a lot of strong personalities in our group. It's good he's here to provide some balance."

She shot a grin over her shoulder. "Give you and Cosette a little break?"

"Exactly." He chuckled quietly, leaning back against the rail. "Of course...he saw you naked on the beach. I guess that means I have to kill him."

She laughed, resting her head against his chest. "I was covered in so much blood, I hardly think it counts. At any rate, I plan on being naked a lot more often."

He froze beneath her, trying hard to think of a suitable response.

"Oh, yeah?" he finally replied. "And why is that?"

She let him hang for a moment before answering with a secret smile. "Because I'm shifting now, silly. What did you think I meant?" She tilted her head, staring up at him innocently. "Guess I should talk to Seth about it. It's a wolf thing."

He lifted his eyebrows and an anticipatory shiver ran up her spine. "Oh, the naked part? You'll just work that out with him?"

She bit down on her lip, trying hard not to smile. "Yeah, probably should."

He nodded slowly, and for a suspended moment neither of them spoke. Then all at once—

"Asher—NO!"

The princess let out a shriek of laughter as the vampire leapt upon her—completely ignoring the fact that they were balanced on a narrow railing above a hundred-foot drop into the sea. His fingers blurred with speed as they tickled her mercilessly, easily deflecting all her half-hearted attempts to break free. At one point he actually dangled her over the side, letting her hang there for a moment before pulling her—breathless—back into his lap.

"Are you insane?!" she shrieked, unable to stop giggling. "We could have *died*!"

He nodded sympathetically.

"Maybe you should get naked. Talk to Seth about it." He shook his head with a grin as she settled back into his arms. "...it's a *wolf* thing."

They sat like that for a while, staring out at the endless water. Then his eyes tightened thoughtfully as he thought back over the events of the last few days.

"Jokes aside...you should have seen the way you two were fighting in the forest. It was perfectly synchronized. Choreographed. Like you were part of the same pack." He glanced down at her with a hint of pride. "I've seen your father fight the same way."

She flushed in surprise.

"Really?"

"Yeah."

There was a little pause.

"But Seth's not in my pack."

Asher laughed quietly.

"You're the Belarian princess. *Everyone* is in your pack." He kissed her softly, pulling back with a tender smile. "It's a shame he has to die."

She laughed again, gazing back across the deck. "I think his heart belongs to someone else."

The two of them watched as Cosette finished with the bow and headed to the pile of weapons to get another. Seth glanced up from a book he wasn't actually reading, aching to go speak with her, but his eyes drifted past to where Ellanden was sharpening a blade on the other side.

The princess vanished up the stairs. He went back to his reading.

"How's Ellanden?" Evie asked quietly, looking back at the fae. At a glance, he appeared to be perfectly normal. One would never suspect he'd been recently stabbed.

"It's painful," Asher answered, following her gaze with a touch of concern. "A lot more painful than he's admitting." He pulled in a breath to say something else, then ended up shaking his head. "It could have been so much worse. The guy took on half the battalion."

Evie's lips twitched with a wry grin. "That's Ellanden."

She could say with absolute certainty that the alternative had never crossed his mind. Why take on just ten Carpathian soldiers when you had a chance to fight so many more?

They lapsed back into silence, staring with affectionate exasperation at their friend. But the longer they sat there, the more troubled the princess became. Yes, Ellanden had fought well on the beach. But it was nothing compared to the savage display she'd seen from the vampire.

Asher *was* the fight.

She stiffened in spite of herself. Trying to remember and forget all at the same time. She wanted to say it was a good thing. He was on their side, after all. Why wouldn't the friends take full advantage of his particular set of skills? And yet...that power had already turned against them.

When he'd attacked Ellanden in the tunnel he'd attacked her, too. Held her completely helpless. Smiled without an ounce of recognition as he prepared to take her blood.

And then there was the bond...

"Babe," she began tentatively, "did you ever—"

"So I've rationed out everything the Carpathians had in the hull," Cosette interrupted suddenly, waving them back down to the deck. The others were already gathered beside her, oblivious to the tense conversation they'd managed to disrupt. "If things hold steady we should have enough for about three weeks, give or take. Given that there probably isn't anything usable in the Dunes, it's going to be a lifesaver. Granted, there's only so much we can carry off the ship."

Evie and Asher slipped noiselessly off the banister, landing beside them.

"The weapons are in order as well," Ellanden added, slinging a massive crossbow across his back. "We can take our pick. Of course, it would help to know what we might be fighting." A shiver swept across his shoulders and he muttered under his breath. "...just want to get this over with."

As if to echo his words, a flash of lightning shot across the sky.

The friends looked up at the same time, staring at the black storm clouds gathering on the horizon. All day long, they'd appeared to be heading south. But as the hours dragged on the winds had shifted, and they looked much closer now than they had before. Already, the temperature was dropping—even more dramatically as they lost the last of the setting sun.

"Let's try to get some sleep," Evie said quietly, fighting a feeling of unease. "With any luck, we'll see land by tomorrow."

Luck? When have we ever had luck?

The others nodded quickly, gathering their things before heading to bed. As Ellanden held open the door they filed below deck, one after another. The princess was the last to go, casting one final look at those troublesome clouds spreading over the sky.

She'd just stepped inside as the first of the raindrops started to fall.

Chapter 6

The princess closed her eyes at midnight and woke up on the deck of the ship. The storm was gone, her friends had vanished, and ripples of silver moonlight were dancing on the crests of the waves.

For a moment, all she could do was stare.

It was beautiful. The ship might have been stolen, the night might have been freezing, and their destination might have been a sprawling wasteland full of the bones of people who'd come before. But it was still beautiful.

She stepped closer to the edge, resting her hands on the railing.

It was only then that she heard them—a chorus of voices coming from somewhere underneath. Her lips curved into a smile as she leaned closer to hear. Such unearthly sounds had never been heard in the halls of men. This was something different. Something less heard than it was felt.

Her body warmed and flushed as the descant rose higher and higher, closing her eyes as it crept into her very soul. She felt as though she could do anything. Her arms lifted as though she might fly.

Then a lone scream shattered the heavenly chorus.

Her eyes shot open and she leaned over the railing, only to see a handful of beautiful people rise up from the depths and float gently upon the waves. Their faces were pale and familiar, their eyes closed in a peaceful slumber. Her friends hadn't vanished after all, they'd simply made their way down into the sea.

The sight of them steadied her, worried her. Filled her a strange tension she didn't understand. She wanted to reach out and touch them, pull them back to the safety of the boat. But they were too far away, resting on the waves.

If only she could get closer—

"Everly."

She lifted her head and saw the one person who hadn't been with the others. The vampire was hovering on the other side of the railing, his feet resting on nothing but air.

"Come with us."

He looked like some kind of angel; light playing with shadows, eyes glowing silver in the moon. The wind picked up and danced around them, blowing strands of dark hair across his face.

The princess stared, transfixed, but was unable to answer. Her feet braced slightly against the deck.

"Come with us," he said again, offering his hand. A flash of lightning tore across the sky, vanishing his skin and illuminating the skull beneath. She recoiled in terror, but it was gone as quickly as it had come. His lips curved up in a gentle smile. "There's nothing to fear. We were mistaken. It's been here all along."

She frowned in confusion, then followed his gaze down to the water. One by one bodies were floating up to the surface, drifting beside her sleeping friends. Only these weren't living. They were only bones.

The lightning flashed again and she let out a piercing scream.

"Wake up!" she cried, desperate to warn them. "Get out of the water!"

Except there wasn't any water. At least, none that she could see. The entire ocean had turned into a skeletal wasteland. The ship was floating upon a sea of bones.

"Come with me..."

Lightning flashed again as torrents of rain plummeted down from the sky. Water poured over the railing of the ship, splashing in freezing puddles around her feet. She could barely see Asher hovering in front of her. Tangles of wet hair were plastered to her forehead and her voice was lost in the howling wind.

"Wake up!" she screamed again, clutching the railing as the ship began to writhe. But her friends were lost in unending slumber—oblivious to churning currents, oblivious to the skeletal fingers curling into their hair.

"Wake up!"

"I tried to warn you," Asher said sadly, still offering his hand. *"Don't say I didn't warn you."*

There was a mighty crash and the ship was violently knocked backwards, throwing the princess off her feet. She scrambled back up in the icy water, grabbing desperately for the railing, just in time to see a giant tentacle slipping back into the sea. A burst of fire exploded above her. A sinister laugh began rumbling underneath—

"WAKE UP!"

Evie opened her eyes with a gasp, bolting upright in bed. Asher was standing exactly where he had been just moments before, but there was nothing of that moonlit angel about him. His eyes were lit with wild panic, and tangles of dark hair clung to the sides of his face.

"It's the storm!" he gasped, barely managing a full sentence. "We kept thinking the wind would have to die down, that it couldn't sustain—" The ship lurched violently and he grabbed the wall for balance, reaching the other hand towards her. "Evie—you've got to come with me!"

Come with me...

She froze a suspended moment, staring at his outstretched hand. Then she leapt out of bed.

"Holy crap!" she gasped as freezing water splashed up her legs. The floor of the cabin was flooded, at least four inches deep. "Asher—are we *sinking*?!"

The torchlight flickered and he grabbed her arm.

"No, I...I don't know. I think that's the rain."

As if on cue, the window carved into the wall burst open—drenching both occupants and everything inside. He let her go for a split second and threw the weight of his body against it, but more water was coming from the other side. Even more was bubbling in from under the door.

Sure...the rain.

She nodded because she wanted to believe him. She nodded because there was literally nothing else to do. Then she grabbed his hand as the two of them battled their way outside.

It wasn't easy. There was trouble at every turn.

Not only was the floor submerged in an ever-rising layer of water, but the ship was rocking violently back and forth—tossing them around like a pair of half-drowned dolls. No sooner would they scramble to their feet than they'd go careening forward again—sliding uncontrollably through the water before crashing into the opposite wall. It was a miracle neither of them lost consciousness. It was a miracle they managed to keep hold of each other's hands.

At one point the churning water reached their waists and Evie lost her footing entirely, vanishing underneath. It was almost a full minute before Asher managed to drag her up again, coughing uncontrollably and disoriented to the point where she could hardly stand.

"Are you okay?!" he gasped, cupping the sides of her face.

She tried to speak, but couldn't. She merely nodded and they took off once again.

Most of the torches had already been extinguished by the time they reached the upper levels of the ship. By the time they got to the final corridor, they were down to the last one.

"There," Asher panted, eyeing the stairwell on the other side, "we made it."

Evie twisted around in his grasp, staring back the way they'd come.

"What about everyone else?" she stammered.

The vampire followed her gaze for only a moment, having tortured himself with the same question every second since he'd stepped inside. "Freya and Ellanden were already on deck when I left to find you. Seth took off to get—"

A gust of wind swept inside, knocking the final torch off the wall. It spluttered into darkness the second it touched the water, vanishing completely with a silent hiss.

STRENGTH

For a second, they both froze.

They had seen the hallway just a moment before. They knew it was deserted. But standing there in the sudden darkness, it was impossible not to imagine all sorts of beasts and terrifying creatures swimming around inside. The hem of Evie's dress brushed against her leg and she jumped a mile. Asher's fangs were digging into his lower lip, filling his mouth with the taste of blood.

Then the moon broke free of the clouds, splintering in through the windows in jagged streaks of light. The hallway was just a hallway. They started moving once more.

Almost there...just a little bit farther...

The ship knocked them forward and they reached the stairs in a full tumble, grabbing the banister and holding on for dear life. After a few seconds, it steadied enough that they were able to get a foothold. They were about to go charging up, when a distant voice reached their ears.

"Hello...? Is anybody there...?"

It was coming from somewhere behind them, so muffled by the storm they could hardly hear. In a dark moment of self-preservation, they were almost tempted to pretend they hadn't heard it. But when it rang out again, they turned to each other at the same time.

"Seth."

They turned around the next instant, abandoning the stairs and charging back down the way they'd come. The water had risen even higher in just the few moments they'd paused, and when Asher tried to yank open the door the countering pressure threw him back against the wall.

"I can't get it!" He gritted his teeth, trying again. "The current's too strong—"

"Then forget the door," Evie interrupted, sloshing her way to the window instead.

Without stopping to think she punched right through the center of it, knocking away the loose shards of glass. The ship tilted dramatically, but she still managed to climb onto the sill before a strong hand yanked her back down.

"What are you doing?!" she demanded, staring up at Asher's face in the dark. "You said he went to find Cosette. They're probably both trapped—"

"Let me go," he interrupted, already pushing past her to the hole. "The ship's taking on water too fast, Evie. I'll go find them. You just get to the deck—"

"Not a chance." She seized the back of his cloak, spinning him around to face her. "That's not what this is, do you understand me?" She emphasized each word. "That's not what this is."

Their eyes met for a brief moment then he nodded.

The two of them made their way carefully out the window before swinging back to the other side. The split second when they were dangling over the roaring sea was bound to give the princess nightmares, but she kept her composure until they'd landed back in the hall. From there, the corridor branched in two directions. And they had no idea which way to go.

"Seth!" she screamed at the top of her lungs, cupping her hands around her mouth. "Seth, can you hear me?"

"Cosette!" Asher shouted beside her, staring down the diverging halls.

There wasn't enough time to check them both. Even if there was, both directions splintered into a dozen other stairwells and chambers—each of which was sure to be flooded by the time they arrived. Unless they had some idea where to go—

"Evie?" a voice called out of the darkness. "Evie—is that you?"

At the same time she and the vampire took off running, abandoning the floor and simply swimming down the hallway when the water got too high. They came to a stop in front of a closed door, staring uncertainly before banging frantically on the other side.

"Seth!" she cried again. "Are you in there? Are you okay?"

There was a muffled splashing, followed by a quiet curse.

"We're here," he answered breathlessly. His voice was much closer, coming from just on the other side of the door. "I found Cosette, but...but the water's rising and we're locked in."

Something in his voice sent chills up the princess' spine.

"What do you mean, you found Cosette—"

Asher pushed her aside.

"Stand back, okay? I'm going to break it down."

There was some more splashing.

"Okay—we're ready!"

The vampire squared his shoulders, then swung at the door with all his might. Instead of breaking through the skin on his knuckles ripped open, staining the water with blood.

"He wasn't kidding," he panted, shaking out his hand. "The whole room must be flooded."

Evie glanced up and down the hall as the water rose to her chest.

"Can you do it?"

"Is it working?" Seth called from inside. "Asher—hurry up!"

The ship creaked precariously beneath them, and the vampire pulled in a breath.

"I don't really have a choice."

Without another moment's pause, he threw himself full-tilt at the door—attacking it with everything he had left, leveraging his full strength against the power of the flood. Evie rushed forward automatically to help him, then took an immediate step back. The force he was using was beyond her capacity. A glancing blow from one of those fists and she wouldn't survive.

It went on long enough that his hands were surely broken, long enough that those waiting on both sides had begun to lose hope. Then all at once, a plank sprang free. The entire door was soon to follow—releasing an ocean of water into the hall.

The princess braced herself with a little shriek, digging both hands into the doorframe until the wave had passed. Only then did she realize how completely the room had actually flooded. At the same time, she waded inside to see Seth and Cosette perched atop the highest shelf.

Seven hells.

Evie sucked in a breath, then froze dead still.

The shifter was staring down at them, but the fae wasn't moving. She was lying in his arms with her head tilted back and her legs dripping streams of water. Those lovely eyes were closed.

"Cosette!" she shrieked, splashing towards them. "Tell me she's not...*Cosette*!"

Seth blinked slowly, as if he was having trouble following along. The image cleared a second later and he shook his head—trying to reassure them.

"She's fine," he panted in complete exhaustion, slipping off the shelf. "She just knocked her head—she's going to be fine."

Evie grabbed the fae's wrists the second they landed, searching for a pulse to be sure. The vampire waded slowly towards them, looking a second away from blacking out himself.

His eyes travelled slowly to the ceiling before returning to Seth. "What were you doing up there?"

The shifter pulled in a shaking breath, glancing down at the girl in his arms.

"Looking for air...we couldn't breathe." It was quiet a moment, then he lifted his head suddenly—staring at each one in turn. "You came back. I didn't...I didn't think you would."

Evie shook her head blankly, crimson hair dripping down her face.

"Of course we came back."

We're in this together.

A sudden hush fell over the four friends, broken only by the noise of the storm. For a moment, they didn't think they could continue. For a moment, it was all too much.

Then the ship creaked again and Evie's heart quickened.

"Come on—we've got to get to the deck."

THE JOURNEY TO THE surface was even harder than the one down. The churning ship was dumping plenty of water back off the side, but no sooner had it righted itself than it filled back up again, sweeping suddenly down the hallway and knocking the friends right off their feet.

The climb out the window to get into the final hallway was especially tricky—even more so given that the water had risen up to their necks. Evie doubled back the second she was through, reaching for Cosette, but Seth refused to part with her. He merely tightened his grip and swung them around to safety, cradling the sleeping princess tight against his chest.

When they finally pushed open the door to the surface, Evie felt as though several lifetimes had passed. But she quickly realized that she was mistaken. The worst was yet to come.

"What the..."

It was if the ocean was exploding. As if her terrifying dream had come to life.

The sky was black, the wind was howling, and the waves were crashing with such ferocity it was a miracle they hadn't already capsized. A second later, she saw the reason why.

Ellanden was rigid as a statue, braced against the deck with such pressure that the heels of his boots had begun to dig into the wood. Both hands were locked against the wheel, using every bit of his strength just to keep it steady, giving his friends they time they needed to make it back.

There was a reason he hadn't come for them. He was busy keeping them alive.

"Landi!" the princess shouted the second they reached the deck.

He jerked his head, but wasn't able to twist around enough to see them. But the second she called, a shadowy figure jumped up beside him—racing towards them across the deck.

"Cosette!"

If it was possible, the witch looked even more concerned than Evie had been herself. She threw herself without restraint onto the weary shifter, trying to pry the fae from his arms.

"What happened?" she shrieked. "Is she breathing?"

As if the questions weren't frantic enough, Ellanden managed to hear them over the storm.

"What...?" He forced his body to turn far enough to see the lifeless princess draped over the shifter's arms. His face froze for a split second, then he forgot the wheel entirely and sprinted full-speed across the deck. "Asher—take it!"

The vampire lifted his head in confusion, then streaked across the ship to take the prince's place—cursing under his breath as he forced his broken hands to grip the massive wheel. A second later, Ellanden appeared in his place—white as sheet when he saw his little cousin.

"What the hell happened!" he cried, wrenching the sleeping girl from the shifter's arms. "I knew I should have gone myself—"

"She knocked her head," Seth murmured, looking like the same thing had happened to himself. When he caught the fae's furious look, he tried again—raising his voice to be heard above the wind. "She knocked her head on the door. She'll be...she'll be fine."

Ellanden caught his breath, but was too worried to tear his eyes from the girl's face. "She had better. For your sake."

Lightning ripped across the sky and the friends lifted their heads, staring breathlessly at the storm. Those black clouds that had been gathering on the horizon were fully upon them, screeching through the wind and roiling the choppy seas. Already, the waves were almost too high for the ship to withstand. Another few feet, and there wouldn't be a ship left to sail.

"What should we do?" Freya blurted, one hand still clamped upon Cosette. "Don't just stand there—say something! What should we do?"

The question hung between them, but no one could find the words. The truth was, everyone had assumed the Dunes would be the treacherous part. No one had considered the voyage at sea.

Another massive wave crashed against the side of the ship, sending the friends careening sideways. The princess manage to catch hold of the opposite rail and stared a frozen moment into the dark waters. For a split second, she could have sworn she saw something—the glint of sea-green eyes hidden amongst the waves. For a split second, she could have sworn someone was staring back.

Then the ship righted itself, spilling them all back upon the deck.

"Asher!" Ellanden yelled. "Hold it steady—"

But there was no point. The second he said the words, a wave rose out of the water unlike any other. One that towered over the little ship, blocking out the night sky.

It hung there for a moment, long enough for Asher to abandon the wheel and streak back to their side. As they stared up at it, one of them, Evie never learned who, asked the fateful question.

"Can everybody swim?"

The princess closed her eyes, grabbing hold of the deck.

Oh shit!

Chapter 7

They say not many people survive a shipwreck.

Those who do are never quite the same. As if the physical component isn't enough, it's the psychological trauma that gets you. Those internal wounds that can never quite manage to heal. The problem is that it's impossible to forget. The moment the waves rise above your head, the moment the deck splinters beneath your feet. Even decades later, people still feel the terror of it—waking up in the middle of the night, drenched in sweat, seeing those images again and again.

Yet others remark that it's a profound experience—a sort of awakening that one can never achieve until facing their own death. Time suspends and sharpens in clarity; memories resurface, awakening secret parts of the soul. They say some people survive the tragedy only to end up craving it for years to come. Chasing after the memory, haunted by the bitter sweetness left in its stead.

Evie woke up with a mouthful of sand.

She would later say that came to summarize her experience.

Am I...dead?

It was a fair question. The princess awoke in a kind of stasis, wedged tightly in a grainy substance her brain couldn't understand. If she'd been recently buried, it would make sense. If giant parts of her body were missing, she wouldn't yet know.

She tried to roll over, then let out a pitiful yelp. That's when she noticed the sand. That's when she pried open her eyes and discovered that she'd face-planted in the middle of a sunny beach.

A *blindingly* sunny beach. Her eyes snapped shut with a wince of pain.

There were noises now. The lazy call of birds, the soft padding of feet. She tried to lift her head. The last thing she wanted as an epilogue

STRENGTH

to her tragic tale was 'the princess was consequently eaten by sand-crabs', but movement was difficult and she decided not to try.

She wanted to throw up, but couldn't. She wanted to pass out, but couldn't.

To make things even harder, someone was lifting her now—fingers were wrapping gently under her arms and pulling her up out of the sand.

"*Seven hells*—she's gorgeous!"

There was a pause.

"I mean...once you get her cleaned up a little."

Another pause. The hands gripping her shifted.

"Run back to camp and tell Rone what happened. I'll deal with this."

"I'll trade you—"

"*Go.*"

The sound of footsteps faded quickly, leaving them in silence. A cheerful voice soon replaced them. One that was smiling, through and through.

"You can wake up now, sweetheart. He's gone."

The princess tried again to open her eyes. Little splinters of light were leaking through. She lifted an arm in an attempt to block them, but it fell lifeless to her side.

Finally, the picture cleared into the face of a man.

She was right about the smile. It was hovering just a few inches above her.

"Welcome back."

In a sudden motion, she flipped onto her side and wretched violently into the sand. Streams of salty water poured from her mouth as her stomach convulsed, ridding itself of whatever was left of the sea. This went on for several minutes, but the man holding her didn't seem to be in any kind of hurry. He simply sat there, rubbing calming circles on her back until she was finally able to catch her breath. She lifted her head slowly, only to see that the smile had remained.

"Where am I?" she asked in a scratchy voice.

It couldn't be the Dunes, could it? They'd come so close—and they were certainly famed for their sand—yet somehow she didn't think so. To start, the Dunes were supposedly deserted, and even if they weren't she highly doubted they'd be occupied by this handsome man with the beaming smile. No, there was no smiling in the Dunes. She had to be somewhere else.

"You, my dear, have washed ashore on the lovely beaches of Haith." His eyes sparkled as she blinked up at him. "Population, well...let's just say your arrival is a welcome surprise."

...washed ashore?

She should have realized this. She was no longer standing on the ship—she should have realized something had changed. But her body was broken and her brain was full of the sea. The last thing she remembered they were standing on deck, watching as a giant wave rose above them.

After that—

"My friends!" She shot up with a gasp, digging her hands into the sand as she attempted to push to her feet. "I have to find—"

He caught her quickly, propping her into a delicate sitting position. As frantic as her attempt had been, she'd only managed to move a few inches. Her legs were still draped across his lap.

"Easy now," he cautioned. "Take a breath—"

"No, you don't understand!" she cried. "There was this wave, and I...I have to find my—"

"Your friends?" he interrupted with a teasing smile. With exaggerated slowness, he rotated them around so she was looking at the rest of the beach. "Congratulations...you found them."

He rubbed his chin thoughtfully, following her gaze.

"Though I can't imagine they're all your friends..."

She didn't hear the last part. Her hand flew to her chest with a choking sob. While there was no telling what condition they might be in, she counted five bodies scattered about the sand. Not one of them had been lost to the ocean—they'd all washed up together on the beach.

Of course, she wasn't the only one who'd noticed them.

"What is this?" she asked quickly. "Who are you people?"

From where she was sitting, very little of it made sense. There were people on the beach, in a very loose sense of the word. Perhaps creatures would have been a better fit.

There was nothing uniform about them.

A group of nymphs was fussing over Cosette, stroking the sides of her face and combing out strands of her long ivory hair. A grizzled dwarf was towering above Ellanden, poking tentatively at his chest with the blunt side of an axe. Seth was the only one who appeared to be stirring, batting blindly at the trio of pixies floating above his head, while a band of what were undoubtedly witches was mothering Freya, murmuring spells and pouring some kind of elixir down her throat.

"Don't do that," the princess murmured, reaching an unseen hand towards them. "Who are those people? What are they giving her?"

The man laughed suddenly, pulling them both to their feet. When she tipped precariously he steadied her, wrapping an arm snugly around her waist.

"So many questions. But I've got one for *you*." He turned suddenly to face her, staring intently into her eyes. "How in seven hells did you wash up on this beach?"

She opened her mouth to answer, still swaying on her feet, but a rush of nerves swept over her and she held her tongue instead. Ships like the one they'd stolen didn't just appear out of nowhere. Nor was it easily forgiven when they were gone. For all she knew, the Carpathians had put a bounty on their heads. And judging by the condition of the straw huts scattered along the beach, these people could certainly use the coin.

"I don't, uh...I don't remember."

His eyebrows lifted in comical disbelief. "Fascinating."

She blanched and pulled away from him. "I'm sorry—I have to check on my friends!"

After two steps, she stumbled. Two more and she was sprawled out on the sand. The man took his time catching up to her, whistling cheerfully as he lifted her to her feet.

"We should probably take this a little slower, don't you think?"

The princess stared up at him in a daze—uncertain whether the emotion she was feeling leaned closer towards gratitude or fear. Her head was spinning and it was hard to make sense of anything whilst being baked by the punishing sunlight. Where were all those lovely storm clouds when she needed them? Where was that inescapable winter chill?

"I'm sorry," she breathed, clutching his arm for balance. "I don't even know your name."

He smiled again, more gently this time.

"It's Eli." His eyes sparkled as he pressed a kiss to the back of her hand. "And you are the most beautiful girl I've ever met."

...what?

She stared back in a dizzy kind of confusion, still trying to figure out if she was awake or if this was a dream. Her hand pulled back ever so slightly, but before she could formulate a proper response a sudden shriek caught her attention from farther down the beach.

The witches who'd been attending Freya had turned their attention to Asher—leaping back the second he opened his eyes. They were quickly joined by a cast of warlocks and shifters, each shouting something in unison, though it was clear the vampire didn't understand.

He looked as dazed as the princess, using every bit of strength just to lift his head off the sand. He flinched when he heard the shouting, blinking quickly as his eyes travelled from face to face. When one of them pulled a knife he scrambled to his feet, only to fall right back down.

Asher.

She couldn't tell if she'd said his name out loud, or merely in her head.

The shouting had escalated and a knife was no longer enough. Instead, the witches stepped forward, lifting their hands and surrounding him in a circle of green light. It got closer and closer as they started chanting, haloing his body as he cringed helplessly in the sand.

"What are you doing...?"

Even so far away, Evie could hear his voice—as frightened and disoriented as her own. He waved his hand slightly, as if he was trying to shake the light loose, then visibly panicked when it started creeping up his arm. His eyes glowed with the reflection as he tried again to stand.

"Please," he panted, unable to catch his breath, "just wait—"

At one point he tried to run, but was kicked back by a towering warlock. At one point the princess tried to call out to him, only to have the notion vanish as soon as it had come.

Time was moving too quickly. The picture flickered on and off.

"What's happening?" she murmured, tilting her head in confusion as they dragged the vampire off the beach and started hauling him into the sea. "What are they doing?"

His legs trailed in the sand behind him. His head bowed limply to his chest. Whatever magic the witches were using had incapacitated him completely. They might as well have used silver chains.

"That's a vampire," Eli responded casually. "They're going to drown it."

Oh, that makes sense.
She nodded along.
Wait...what?!
"STOP!"

She wrenched herself free and took off running in the same instant—falling down several hundred times in the sand. As far as rescue attempts went, it was truly pathetic. But it managed to catch the attention of the people trying to force the vampire's head under the waves.

"Is she serious?"

"Poor girl's gone mad with the sun."

The nymphs shook their heads disapprovingly as she stumbled towards them. The witches turned around in alarm. Asher himself couldn't seem to see past the neon light deadening his body, but his face lifted almost as if he could sense she was there.

"Evie...?"

She reached the water just as a shifter grabbed a fist of the vampire's hair and forced his head under. She threw up her hands in horror as he thrashed helplessly beneath the waves.

Then she let out a piercing cry as a wave of liquid fire shot from her palms.

The beach suddenly fell silent. The vampire surfaced with a gasping breath.

There were a few moments where no one said anything. A crowd had gathered. Her friends were amongst them, staring breathlessly from the sand. The princess stared in astonishment at her smoking fingers before hiding them quickly behind her back. Her cheeks flushed and her knees were shaking. She lifted her eyes slowly to the rest of them, trying to think of something to say.

"Total. Accident."

She raised her hands in surrender.

Then she fainted dead away.

Chapter 8

The first thing Evie noticed was the smell.

It clung to every surface, creeping up her nostrils and seeping into her pores. It was something familiar, something overpoweringly sweet. But she wasn't able to place it better than that. The next thing she noticed was the heat. It might have been winter elsewhere in the realm, but no one had told the good people of Haith. Whatever bits of skin that lay exposed were sizzling under its rays, the rest of her drenched in sweat.

The last thing she heard was a donkey. That's when she decided to open her eyes.

What the—?

Her hands were tied and she was lying in back of what looked like an old feed cart, bumping along beneath a canopy of trees. About a thousand sunbaked fruits were rattling around beside her, jumping into the air every time the wheels of the wagon hit a deep groove in the road. A man was sitting in the front, holding the reins. Another man was sitting beside him. Neither seemed at all concerned with their passenger. Neither was turned enough that she could see a face.

There were many questions to be asked, many quiet mysteries that needed to be answered. But she settled on what she took to be the most pertinent one.

"...are those mangos?"

There was sudden movement beneath her—something she'd thought was part of the wagon until it pulled in a breath. She lifted her eyes slowly, squinting painfully into the sun, only to be met with the most condescending expression the five kingdoms had ever seen.

"Of course you ask about the fruit."

Nobody does sarcasm like the Fae.

"Ellanden!"

She peeled her cheek off his shirt, forcing her arms into a clumsy embrace. The rope around her wrists made it difficult, but the prince had no restraints. He held her tight against his chest.

"I'm *really* glad you woke up," he breathed, pressing an unexpected kiss to her hair.

From the looks of things, she was the only one. The rest of the friends were sprawled in similar states of dishevelment across the feed truck, bouncing obliviously with the mangos as the wagon and its mysterious drivers carried them further and further into the trees.

None of them appeared to be seriously injured, but it was impossible to know for sure. The only thing that kept the princess from panicking was that Ellanden wasn't panicking himself.

Then again, maybe that wasn't an accurate gauge. The man looked *exhausted*.

Far from his usual radiance, the fae was tired and pale. His face was bruised, his ivory hair hung in matted tangles, and there was a wilt to his shoulders she had never seen before. Strange crescent-shaped marks trailed down the side of his chest, and while he was embracing her tightly it was only with one arm. The other was hanging motionless by his side.

"Do you remember what happened?" she whispered, glancing covertly at the men driving the cart. "Do you have any idea how we got here?"

His face stilled for a moment, then he shook his head.

"Not really...just fragments. I remember the ship splitting down the middle—us getting thrown into the water. I think maybe I was caught in something..."

He trailed off, an uncertain emotion troubling his eyes.

The princess understood completely. She remembered other things—sorting the arrows, rescuing the others below deck. But when she tried to think back to shipwreck itself, there was a massive gap in her memory—like someone had meticulously carved it right out of her brain.

"I've never heard of Haith," Ellanden continued suddenly. "The only one who might have is Seth, but he still hasn't woken up. But I do know that this," he glanced up at the blinding sun, "is nowhere near where we were. I don't understand how we could have gotten here."

Or how we're going to get back across that sea...

Evie considered this for a moment, then decided to take charge of morale.

"We're lucky we washed up here," she answered with a false sense of cheer. "These people seem friendly enough...even if they were a little enthusiastic with that rope."

"Lucky?" Ellanden laughed shortly. "Tell that to Asher."

All at once, the images came flooding back.

How the witches had imprisoned him in that strange green light. How the rest of the beach had formed an impromptu lynch mob, dragging him off towards the sea.

He was propped up on the other side of the wagon—strands of damp, sandy hair tangled across his face. His eyes were closed, but there didn't appear to be any lasting damage from the spell.

He and the princess were the only ones to have been tied with rope.

"Here," Ellanden murmured, as if reading her thoughts, "let me get that."

With a single hand, he worked the knots loose—tossing the rope over the side of the cart when he was finished. The drivers didn't notice. Judging by their level of careless supervision, Evie doubted they would even care. She rubbed gingerly at her wrists, still staring at Asher.

"I thought he was awake," she whispered. "I remember seeing—"

"He passed out after you did," Ellanden interrupted softly. "Fell right back into the water, only this time the witches actually pulled him out."

"Why would they...?"

She trailed off as another memory floated to the surface, one that was a bit more fire-and-brimstone than anything she'd had planned. A delayed jolt of astonishment swept over her as she stared down at her palms, suddenly understanding why the villagers had tied her hands.

That was real? I actually did that?

"Your little fire show on the beach saved his life." Ellanden glanced down with the hint of a smile. "Mommy dearest would be proud."

She simply shook her head, at a loss for what to say. Perhaps Freya was right. Perhaps magic could only grow in times of great need. The moment she'd thought Asher was about to die?

She didn't think she'd ever needed it more.

The wagon bumped again, tossing them against the wooden rails. There was some laughter from the front of the cart. Good-natured laughter, but the fae leaned back with a roll of his eyes.

"That being said, I've had better accommodations."

She pursed her lips to hide a smile. Knowing the fae, she wasn't sure what offended him more. That he was in a feed cart, or that he hadn't been allowed to drive.

"I talked with them a little," he continued, stretching his legs stiffly in front of him. "They promised us food and medical attention. I'm not sure whether I believe them, but at this point I scarcely see the harm. We would have died if they'd left us on the beach."

Judging by the temperature alone, she couldn't disagree. Little heat waves were shimmering above every surface of the wagon. The fruit crammed on the bottom layer was starting to rot.

She nodded at the rest of them, and one in particular.

"Should we try to get them up—"

There was no need. No sooner had she spoken the words than the trees cleared suddenly and the wagon came to an abrupt stop. The donkey turned its head and immediately began eating the underbrush, while the drivers dismounted, circled round, and pulled open the back of the cart.

"Hello again!"

Evie stared back warily at the man she'd met on the beach. He was still smiling, it seemed his natural state, though it hardened a bit when he saw Ellanden's arm wrapped around her waist.

"This is your camp?" the fae asked, trying to see past him.

Eli nodded slowly, glancing over his shoulder.

"It's nearby. We thought you might want to get cleaned up first. Get some of that fruit juice off your clothes before something out here mistakes you for lunch."

Evie glanced reflexively at her dress before staring out towards the trees.

They were thicker than the ones she was used to—with narrow trunks, spindly branches, and wide balmy leaves. Nothing like the tall oaks and evergreens that surrounded the palace. The flowers were different, too; brighter colors, sharper smells. No doubt the animals had evolved to suit them.

"Like what—" she started to ask, then caught herself. "Thank you."

Eli smiled again, gesturing to the road.

"Thank *you*. We're pretty hard up for entertainment around these parts." His eyes twinkled as they swept over the cart. "And something tells me you've got quite a story to tell..."

WHAT STARTED AS AN outdoor bath in a natural spring turned into an unintentional joke. The friends cleaned up as best they could—ducking their heads beneath the warm water and scrubbing vigorously at their clothes—but the second they toweled off they found themselves wet all over again. The humidity was so intense, clouds of steam hung heavy over the slick stone. It soaked their hair and dampened their skin, making it flat out impossible to keep anything dry.

"You're looking a great deal better," Eli called from the shore. He'd been watching them with his partner, who'd yet to say a word. When he caught their silent stares, he amended the initial assessment. "At least you're clean…"

The others returned to their work, but Asher continued watching him—wringing out his shirt with a slight frown on his face. "What's his name again?"

"Eli," the princess murmured, extracting a piece of driftwood from her hair. "He was the guy who found me on the beach."

The vampire glanced between them, then nodded in silence.

There was much to discuss. Not the least of which was how in the world his girlfriend had managed to shoot liquid fire from her hands. But they would get to it in time. For now, the friends had more immediate concerns. Like where exactly that cart was taking them.

"Are you nearly finished?" Eli called again, tapping his foot impatiently. "I suggested that you rinse off, there isn't time to preen."

"Oh, he's a darling," Ellanden muttered, sloshing past them towards the shore.

Evie laughed quietly, glancing back at Asher as she followed suit. "You coming?"

"Yeah," he answered quietly, his eyes still on their drivers. "Right behind you."

The vampire hadn't said much since waking up in the back of the cart. Blame it on the lynch mob who'd tried drowning him fangs-first in the sea, but he was keeping mostly to himself.

His eyes told a whole other story. Screaming silent warnings the others would never see.

Together, the six friends trudged to shore and started following their cheerful guide as he led them on a winding trail through the dense trees.

"It's like hiking in a steam bath," Cosette murmured, panting slightly as she hurried to keep up with the others. "I can't believe it's still winter."

Seth fell into step beside her, extracting a tiny snake that had fallen unnoticed into her hair.

"The storm blew us far off course," he said vaguely, though it sounded like he didn't have any better recollection than they did themselves. "I'm sure we'll find answers soon enough. And in the meantime...who doesn't like a steam bath?"

The fae laughed in spite of herself, glancing up to meet his gaze. They stared for a moment, about to say more, when the witch pushed obliviously in between them, stomping through the ferns.

"Screw the storm, I agree with Cosette." She slapped the side of her neck, wondering if there were giant bugs in the world after all. "How can anyone live like this—"

A second later, her question was answered. Because a second later, they reached the camp.

Evie's eyes widened as the path they were following abruptly ended, revealing a massive clearing cut into the very heart of the trees. It was extraordinary. A jungle oasis, hiding in plain sight.

How did the villagers deal with the heat?

They didn't. They simply took off their clothes.

Not all of them, of course. But enough to make the village a sight to behold. Instead of fabric, they wore intricately-woven bands of leather, carefully positioned to cover only what was necessary, while leaving everything else on full display. Some of the men wore pants, but nothing further. Some of the women were bedecked in little more than what Evie and the others wore to swim at the palace back home. Bright feathers and clawed jewelry adorned both men and women alike, and everyone—from the elders to the children—was strangers to the idea of shoes.

There was no real structure, nothing more than a communal well and a scattering of straw-roofed huts. The entire thing looked more like a permanent campsite than a village—though the people who resided there had certainly made it a home. Those brightly-colored flowers that littered the forest were everywhere, sprouting from empty barrels and draped decoratively over doors. Little gardens had been planted behind some of the larger huts, and the grass in the center of the clearing had been cleared away to make room for what looked to be a massive fire-pit dug into the earth.

The princess' lips parted with a look of silent wonder. It was as if they'd stumbled upon some kind of ancient tribe, untouched by the modern world.

But how is that possible, she thought, looking at the wide variety of creatures milling about in the tall grass. *And why do so many different races live together, unless...*

Her eyes lit up in sudden understanding.

They're Kreo.

Ellanden took an involuntary step forward, lips parting with surprise.

"I've been here before," he breathed. "Or at least, somewhere like it." A group of shrieking children raced past, bringing a little smile to his face. "My gran had a place like this. I used to go there every summer."

Gran?

It wasn't like the fae to be so informal. In fact, the only time he spoke in such casual terms was when dealing with this side of his heritage—the side he'd chosen to repress.

Most of the others knew better than to push things further. One of them did not.

"Gran?" Seth repeated curiously, finding the term as jarring as the rest. "You come from a place like this?"

It was impossible to hide the doubt in his voice, and the princess wasn't sure if the fae would be offended. The fae wasn't sure himself. He merely answered in a quiet voice.

"My mother's side."

"Of course..." Seth murmured, putting it together for the first time. A second later he lit up, staring around the village with sudden excitement. "Wait, but wouldn't that make you—"

"Quiet, shifter," Ellanden said sharply. "Not another word."

Seth's eyes cooled sarcastically, though the excitement remained.

"Right, because you wouldn't want any of these people to know you're their—"

Ellanden clamped a hand over his mouth, eyes burning. "No, I wouldn't. I'm serious, Seth. Not a single word."

The shifter raised his eyebrows but held his tongue. At the same time, Eli detached from the man who'd driven beside him and doubled back to the group.

"Wait here for a moment...I'll send for you soon."

The friends watched in silence as he made his way through the camp.

They were standing within the tree-line and had gone generally unnoticed. Life in the little village continued as it always had. Screaming children ran back and forth—playing war games with painted faces. Clusters of nymphs and witches lounged together along the edges of the clearing, weaving long pieces of grass into baskets and basking in the filtered sun.

A strange assortment of people was gathered in the center—their heads bent together as they discussed something the rest of the camp was obviously not supposed to hear. Eli headed straight towards them, joining the tight-knit ring and muttering under his breath.

There were several exclamations, several looks of surprise. At one point, Evie could have sworn she heard the word *vampire*.

Asher took a step backwards, poised to run. He had not forgotten his first encounter with the angry mob. There would not be a second. The others tensed alongside him, ready to flee at a moment's notice. But before any such drastic measures could be taken, a heavy-set dwarf in the center muttered a few choice words and the others roared in laughter. When they dispersed, they were still smiling. Eli appeared amongst them, waving the friends into camp.

"We've been given approval," Ellanden said with a touch of surprise. "They won't harm us—the decision is set."

"Set by whom?" Freya asked excitedly, stretching on her toes for a better view.

"That's a very good question," Seth murmured, looking far more cautious than the young witch. "Do they have a king or something?"

Ellanden tensed ever so slightly.

"They have a chief."

Evie and Asher exchanged a quick look, while Freya bounced eagerly between them.

"How do you know which one he is?"

The fae laughed humorlessly. "Trust me...we'll know."

As he spoke, an old man detached from the others. There was nothing particularly regal about him, nothing that would distinguish him save his rather extraordinary age. Perhaps the only thing that gave it away was the confidence with which he walked towards them.

And the dead bat plastered atop a driftwood crown.

Yep—that looks about right.

"Welcome, children!" He spread his arms wide, inadvertently mimicking the deceased animal mounted upon his brow. "I sent people to the beach for mangos, and look what they brought back instead. What a strange collection of travelers..."

Us? Evie's eyebrows lifted into her hair. *You're calling us strange?*

"The vampire was travelling with them." An oily warlock who'd been there on the beach spoke up behind him. "We found him lying in the sand."

Asher stiffened involuntarily, positioned deliberately in the middle of his friends.

"Yes, I can see that," the chief said calmly, never breaking his gaze. He stared a long time at the young vampire, seeing things the others could not. "I met a civilized vampire once. He was something of an enigma, travelling from place to place, trying to unite in harmony what was left of his kind. In all my years, I'd never seen anything like it."

His gaze sharpened in sudden intensity.

"In all my years, there was only ever the one."

Evie's eyes flew to Asher, but the vampire was maintaining a careful calm. All his life, he'd lived in the shadow of his people's reputation. Whatever look the chief was giving him, he'd seen it before. But the chief was giving him something else—an opportunity. He wasn't going to waste it.

In a move that forever won the princess' respect, he offered his hand with a smile.

"Now you've met two."

A hush fell over the camp as every creature living within the trees stared breathlessly at the two men. The silence went on loud and long, but Asher never faltered. He simply kept his hand between them—waiting for the chief to either accept it or not.

At which point...we run.

The old man stared at him a second more, then he did the one thing less likely than shaking hands with a civilized vampire. He embraced him.

"In that case...you are *most* welcome."

The friends let out a collective breath, as the warlock spat in the dirt behind him. Asher was visibly relieved, yet hyper-aware of the bat at the same time. He pulled away carefully, eyes flickering up to it while he fought to keep a smile on his face.

"Thank you," he murmured, uncomfortable with all the attention. "We didn't mean to press your hospitality, my friends and I were shipwrecked at sea—"

"And I'm sure that's a fascinating tale," the chief interrupted. "But you won't be telling it now. Save it for tonight. We're throwing a feast."

"A feast?" Evie blurted without thinking. "You really don't have to—"

"Nonsense." The chief's eyes twinkled as he looked them up and down. "It isn't often we get visitors, let alone some who've washed up on our shores. A warm supper is the least we can do."

A ripple of excitement swept over the village as those close enough to have heard the proclamation quickly spread the news to the others.

"In the meantime sleep, rest, gather your strength." The chief's voice softened as he gestured around the camp. "You're safe now. No one will harm you."

The friends stared back in silence, waiting for the other shoe to drop. When nothing happened, they all began speaking at once—thanking him profusely as he sauntered away.

"A feast, huh?" Seth gave the prince a pointed nudge. "They don't seem so bad to me."

Ellanden ignored him, walking stiffly to the nearest vacant hut.

The princess stared cautiously after him, but she couldn't help but agree with Seth. Of all the welcomes they'd received over the last few weeks, a feast certainly ranked top of the list.

Double or nothing, it's going to be mangos.

Chapter 9

As it turned out, the Kreo settlement was a lot more expansive than it had originally seemed. Only a few central houses were in the grassy clearing, the rest of them were hidden in the trees.

Not amongst the trees...but *inside* them.

"This is incredible," Evie breathed, peering once more outside her window.

It was like they'd entered some kind of puzzle, an elaborate labyrinth of twisting rope bridges that led from one magnificent treehouse to the next. Her mother once told her she'd been to a settlement like it—when she'd met Ellanden's great-grandmother for the first time. She'd gushed about the warmth and vibrancy before muttering something about a deranged panther and turning in early for bed. As usual, Evie selectively remembered only the parts she wanted to hear, but even after having imagined such a place for so many years...the reality was blowing her mind.

"Why did Ellanden never take us with him?" she murmured almost to herself. "He went for the beginning of every summer, but he always made it sound like such a drag."

On the one hand, she could almost see why. The steamy Kreo jungle was nothing like the ivory palace the prince called home. Between the mud, the dwarves, and the inherently imperious nature of a fae she could see him being resistant to the idea. Throw in a dead bat or two and he might flat-out refuse. But she'd seen something else on his face when he watched those children running by. The same tender nostalgia as when he'd smelled the wildflowers for the first time.

Like it or not—a part of this was home.

"I think he was embarrassed," Cosette replied, coming to stand beside her at the window. "I remember asking him what it was like once when we were kids, but he wouldn't really say. Just that it was hot and loud— everything you might expect from people who decorated themselves in bones."

Evie laughed under her breath. "Yeah, that sounds like Ellanden."

"But I know he missed it when he came back to Taviel," Cosette added suddenly. "I walked in on him chanting one time—holding this weird necklace in his hand. He stuffed it under his bed and threatened to cut off my hair if I ever told anyone."

The princess rolled her eyes with a smile. "That sounds like him, too."

"I don't know what in the world he'd be embarrassed about," Freya exclaimed, examining herself in the mirror. "This is hands-down the greatest place I've ever seen!"

The young witch had fully embraced the lifestyle of the Kreo—more specifically the wardrobe. The second they closed the door of their room, she ripped off her clothes and began adorning herself with the same leather bands the rest of them wrapped around their bodies. A generous selection of clawed jewelry was soon to follow. She could no longer find her shoes.

Both Evie and Cosette wanted very much to tease her.

Except they'd done the exact same thing.

How scandalized they'd be at the palace, if anyone could see them. The two princess of the High Kingdom decked out like jungle gladiators. Their old governess would faint dead away.

"I won't say it's comfortable...but it's easy to move around in." Cosette sliced her arms in a wide circle, mimicking the motions of shooting a bow. "I could definitely hunt in this."

Evie laughed, while Freya rolled her eyes—shoving the fae onto a chair so she could begin braiding her hair. "Yeah, because that's *totally* what the Kreo had in mind when they started wearing these things. That it would be easier to hunt."

Evie pursed her lips, fiddling with the claws hanging from her neck. "They were probably thinking it was stiflingly hot—"

Freya held up a hand, unwilling to listen. Instead she turned her full attention to the fae, twisting tiny braids into her long hair. "Seth was looking at you again today."

Cosette visibly tensed, looking away from the mirror.

"Seth almost drowned like the rest of us," she said dismissively. "He's probably just thanking the gods he's still alive—"

"He'll be thanking them for a little more than that when he sees you in this tonight," Freya interrupted coyly, putting the final touches to the fae's hair. "In fact, I'd be *very* surprised if he doesn't ask to come back to your room."

Evie snorted with laughter, while Cosette's face went cold.

"Silence, witch."

"I'm just saying—"

"Perhaps if you spent more time on your own dalliances, you'd realize that Ellanden *wasn't* looking at you. He never does. And I highly doubt that ferret you're wearing will change that."

Freya's eyes flashed in anger before she glanced suddenly at the bones circling her wrist. "Wait...this was a ferret?"

And that's my cue to leave.

Evie slipped out while they were still arguing, shutting the door silently behind her. The sun had set about an hour before and torches had been lit along the swinging pathway. She wandered aimlessly for a while before coming to a place she remembered from when Eli had escorted them to their chambers. While all of the friends were sharing a room, Asher had been given one of his own.

She knocked lightly on the door, listening intently to the other side. It was no use. There was no way of tracking a vampire once they decided to move. One moment Asher was standing thoughtfully by the window, the next he was standing in the frame.

"Everly."

It came out as almost a gasp as he looked her up and down. His eyes dilated slightly, resting on certain parts before returning almost feverishly to her face.

For a long moment, they just stood there. Then the princess cleared her throat.

"...can I come in?"

He flushed with embarrassment and pulled open the door. "Of course. Sorry."

She swept past him, secretly thrilled with his reaction but trying awfully hard to act casual. His room looked very much the same as hers, minus the teenage girls threatening each other with bodily harm. The window opened onto a stunning view of the jungle, a warm breeze swaying the trees.

"I didn't mean to surprise you." She turned around to face him. "I just wanted to..." Her gaze fell on the Kreo clothes still lying on his bed. "...get you for the feast."

A single look at his face said it all.

"You're not coming, are you?"

He hesitated, worried about disappointing her, then shook his head with a sigh. "I don't think anyone would like to see me there—vampire at a feast. Besides," he glanced down at himself self-consciously, "I'm not really in the best state."

When the friends had arrived at the camp, none of them was at their best. If it wasn't the injuries they'd sustained in the shipwreck and from the Carpathians before, most all of them had suffered from mild heatstroke upon washing up on the beach. Fortunately, the resident coven of witches had cured such maladies with a healing elixir. Unfortunately, the vampire couldn't partake.

The princess bypassed her first question to ask her second.

"Wait—what do you mean? What's wrong with you?"

Before he could answer she swept forward, lifting her fingers to the hem of his shirt. He stiffened slightly as she rolled it up his stomach, pulling it over his head with a gasp.

"Asher..."

There wasn't an inch of him that wasn't marked—whether it be bruises, or lacerations, or the kind of discoloration that made her wonder if the witches' light had burned his skin. Beyond that, there was everything you'd expect to find from a survivor of a shipwreck. Plus a little more.

"It isn't that bad," he deflected quickly, grabbing unsuccessfully for his shirt.

She ignored him completely, running the tips of her fingers over his skin. "Why aren't these healing?"

He tried to shrug, but it was too painful. Instead, he simply picked up his shirt.

"I'm sure they will," he said evasively. "It's just taking a little longer."

He was about to add something stupid, like, 'maybe it's the heat'. But his girlfriend wasn't like most people. She'd grown up around vampires. His lies and deflections seldom worked.

Her eyes traveled twice between his chest and the dark circles under his eyes before lighting with sudden understanding. "You need to feed."

He shook his head, trying to stop her.

"Hang on—"

"What are you waiting for?" she interrupted, grabbing him by the hand. "It's a *feast*, Ash. I'm sure they'll have something."

"I don't need—"

"I don't care how weird you are about eating in front of other people." She towed him towards the door. "These people are weird, too, all right? This is no time to be squeamish."

"Evie, stop—"

"Quit stalling." She yanked open the door. "We're going to be—"

He slammed it shut again, wrenching himself free.

"I'm not going to the feast!"

She blinked up at him, falling quiet.

"Evie, I..." He moved away from her, too ashamed to look her in the face. "This isn't healing because I need something stronger."

Silence fell between them, broken only by the princess' quiet, "...oh."

Her mother had spoken of this as well. The blood of animals could only sustain a vampire; it wasn't powerful enough to heal, not when it came to injuries as grave as these. With a spike of panic, she suddenly wondered why Asher didn't want to go to the feast. Was he worried about the way people might look at him? Or was he worried about the way they might look to him?

A ripple of fear washed over her. But she squared her shoulders and looked into his eyes.

"So drink something stronger."

He stared for a moment before his face whitened with shock. "...what?"

They had done it once before. Only once. And only to resurrect him from the brink of death after a kelpie had tried to drown him in a river. To suggest doing it again?

"Evie, this *will* get better," he said hastily, snatching the shirt from her hands and sliding it back over his head. "It will just take—"

"Time?" she finished sarcastically. "Time that we *don't* have?"

He shook his head quickly, avoiding her eyes. "This isn't casual—"

"And I'm not offering casually," she interrupted again, stepping towards him. "You need help, Asher. Let me help you."

Their eyes met for a split second, then he turned away.

"I...I can't," he said quickly. Too quickly. His eyes had flickered to her neck. "We've talked about stuff like this before. You know that I'd never—"

"You already have," she said plainly, sweeping her hair off her neck. When he didn't move, she let out a theatrical sigh. "Look, I'm just going to stand here until you do it, so you might as well not make us late for the feast. They might have kabobs."

He stared at her a moment, then laughed in spite of himself. The curtains fluttered as he closed the distance between them, wrapping a hand behind her head. A shiver swept across her skin as he leaned closer. Her eyes fluttered shut and she pulled in a breath.

...then he pressed a gentle kiss to her neck.

"I don't have to do it there," he said softly. "It's more painful." He reached down and took her hand, smoothing it flat with a conflicted expression. "Are you *sure*?" At this point, he was talking to himself as much as her. His eyes swept over her soft skin, and he shook his head slightly. "I don't want to do this..."

"You don't have a choice," she answered quietly, lifting her wrist. "Come on. Drink." She paused suddenly as an unexpected truth rose to the surface. "...I want you to."

His eyes flashed up with a heated expression, locking onto hers in the dark. Another prickle of fear danced across her skin but she lifted her wrist even higher, pressing it to his lips.

A second later, she felt his fangs.

They sliced cleanly through her skin, puncturing a vein as his lips closed in a dark sort of kiss. Her head swam immediately when she felt the sudden pressure, but this time she kept her eyes wide open—determined to feel every bit of it.

It wasn't like she had a choice. It was pure sensation.

Her breathing hitched as he drank deeper, wrapping his other hand instinctively around her arm. A warm tingling sensation followed his every move, hooking deep in her stomach as she took a step closer, winding her fingers through his dark hair.

His eyes closed with a quiet moan and things started moving faster.

She was suddenly aware of his clothes. She was suddenly aware of her own. She suddenly wanted, very much, to take them all off. Asher seemed to be thinking the same thing.

Without ever breaking their connection, he started walking backwards—leading them to the bed. She stumbled after him, a willing prisoner, climbing on top of him as he lay down.

The tug on her wrist became sharper. The tingling faded and her arm began to go numb.

The world tilted suddenly as Asher flipped them over—pressing her into the mattress so he was lying on top. His teeth dug in with a little growl, but his hands never stopped moving. They fought briefly with the leather straps of her new shirt before tearing clean through them and tossing it to the floor. Her pants were soon to follow. His clothes were already gone.

This is happening. I can't believe—

Her head spun suddenly and she pushed weakly against his chest. "Ash…"

He stopped at once, pulling back with his mouth dripping red. The sight of it was enough to startle her out of her trance. She leaned back with a shiver. A second later she picked up her shirt.

"I'm sorry," he said quickly, lifting a hand to cover his fangs. "Evie, I didn't mean to—"

"It's fine," she said just as fast, wishing that for once he wasn't able to hear the erratic pounding of her heart. "We should get to the feast. We don't want to be late."

He froze for a moment, naked and panting, then pushed off the bed in one lithe motion, sweeping his own clothes off the floor. She shot a secret look at him in the mirror.

His skin was already healed. Hers would take longer.

They dressed quickly and headed for the door—drowning in the silence, unable to say a word. A second before she could pull it open he stepped in front, staring in a quiet panic.

"Please tell me we're okay," he begged. "I didn't realize that was going too far. I thought this was always the plan. I mean, we had talked about it..."

When she didn't say anything, that panic increased tenfold.

"Evie, I *never* would have done anything if I thought you didn't want to—"

She shook her head quickly, eyes prickling with secret tears.

"It wasn't too far. It was fine. Let's just...let's just get to the feast, okay?"

He stared a moment longer then stepped silently out of the way, holding open the door as she slipped outside. The evening breeze chilled her flushed skin, and for the first time since arriving at the village she wished she was wearing more clothes.

"After you," Asher said quietly, gesturing to the path with a lifeless smile.

She rushed past him, wiping a secret tear as she started to cry.

The problem wasn't that she hadn't wanted to.

The problem was that she had.

Chapter 10

By the time Evie and Asher made it to the clearing, the feast had already started.

Several wide tables had been dragged into the center of the grass, sagging with the weight of every imaginable kind of food. And what looked like the entire village was gathered noisily around them—eating, laughing, and drinking without a care in the world.

Eli hadn't been exaggerating when he'd implied there weren't many of them. The entire community could fit into a single wing of her father's palace. Evie studied them carefully, well aware that she was being studied herself.

There were several obvious standouts—nixies, pixies, dwarves, and a handful of nymphs that were emblems of the supernatural community and impossible to hide. From what she knew about the magical heritage of the Kreo, she was guessing the rest of them was an assortment of witches, warlocks, and shifters. Witches, in particular, seemed to dominate the rest of the group.

It might have been a limited community, but it was a happy one.

A pair of young men with fiddles weaved their way casually throughout the party, pausing every now and then to steal a sip of wine. Old dwarves gulped ale with their beards dragging on the ground, while all the children who'd been playing were now dancing around the roaring bonfire, throwing in handfuls of pinecones and shrieking with delight at the accompanying shower of sparks.

Given the parade of horrors to which the friends had become accustomed, it was like coming up for a breath of fresh air.

Then why am I still shaking?

The princess spotted her friends immediately and made a bee-line right for them. Even amidst the colorful assortment of company, they tended to stand out. Perhaps because Freya was doing her best imitation of a Carpathian warlord. Perhaps because Ellanden was the only person at the entire party who was still stubbornly wearing shoes.

Evie flashed a quick smile and sat down beside him, pretending not to notice as Asher seated himself in silence on the opposite side of the table. They hadn't spoken since leaving his room. Not a single word. It was new territory for them. The fae would prove a natural buffer.

"Really getting into the spirit of things, are we?" she teased.

Ellanden flashed her a cold look. "Not all of us must pretend to be savages." But he did a double-take in spite of himself. "You look hot."

She laughed shortly, relieved to be back on familiar ground. "Thanks."

Seth lowered his voice conspiratorially, leaning across the table. "The fae might not have embraced the wardrobe, but he does approve of the whiskey." He picked up a flagon and poured the princess a glass. "I've been told you'll feel the same."

She picked it up gratefully, throwing it back like a shot. "Keep them coming..."

Unlike the fae the shifter had immersed seamlessly into Kreo culture, and she had to say it suited him very well. He was topless save for a pair of leather bands around his arms, and his tanned skin glowed like honey in the light of the fire. Two crimson suns had been painted on his chest and his dark hair was strung with decorative braids, brushing the tops of his shoulders.

She smiled in spite of herself, pointing at the suns. "Please tell me you've had those the entire time."

He laughed, glancing over his shoulder at the children. "Just wait—they'll get you, too. They're impossible to resist."

They're not the only ones...

Cosette had abandoned her seat at the table and was dancing with the children in a circle around the fire. Long gone was the stoic warrior who tracked down ancient monsters and rescued her friends from the wizard's cage. For once, the young princess looked exactly as Evie remembered. Breathless with laughter, dancing barefoot by the fire. Flowers in her hair, starlight in her eyes.

Seth was spellbound. He distracted himself as best he could—pouring drinks for the others and making stabs at conversation, but not a full minute could pass without him glancing reflexively over his shoulder. He could have watched her for hours, long after the party was over and the rest of them had gone to bed. Evie followed his gaze, then leaned conspiratorially across the table.

"How goes your crusade?"

He jumped slightly, quickly turning back around. It might have caused more of a stir, but the party was loud and the friends had all been drinking. *Heavily*.

"Things are progressing according to schedule," he answered casually. "I'm in the invisible stage now—where I pine away in silence and she occasionally forgets I'm alive."

Despite her own flailing crusade, the princess couldn't help but laugh. It was one of the things she loved most about shifters—they were adorably candid. This one more than most.

Of course, not everyone agreed.

"I suggest you keep it that way," Ellanden said lightly, watching a pair of nymphs over the rim of his glass. "Invisible is a good look on you. No need for things to change."

A faint blush appeared on Seth's cheekbones, while Evie tipped her drink into the fae's plate.

"Hey, you finally made it!" Freya rejoined them suddenly, landing with a grin in the chair on Ellanden's other side. She downed what was left of his whiskey, slamming down the empty glass with a flourish. "What took you guys so long? I was about to go looking for you."

There was an imperceptible pause.

"We got lost," Asher lied easily, managing a little smile while the princess gulped whiskey behind him. "Those rope bridges all look the same."

Freya nodded distractedly, but Ellanden glanced between them with the hint of a frown. The princess deliberately ignored him. The same way she eased her arms casually beneath the table when his eyes flickered to her wrists.

"Not much incentive for a vampire to go to a feast anyway, right?"

The others glanced up in surprise and Seth froze in embarrassment.

Despite the obvious effort he was making, the man had spent the majority of his life in a world where heroes were a thing of the past and vampires were a daily threat. It was still difficult to reconcile with the fact that one member of their group came equipped with a pair of fangs and the strength of the undead. When Asher had sat unthinkingly beside him, he'd tensed in his chair.

The group stared in silence and he back-pedaled quickly.

"I only meant—"

"It's fine," Asher said dismissively. "I know what you meant."

Normally, the shifter would have changed the subject. Any sane person would have done the same. But there was nothing normal about their circumstances. They were sharing a quest, they were sharing a table, and he was more than a little drunk. In a burst of recklessness that would baffle him the following morning he leaned closer, examining the vampire for the first time.

"I'm sorry they tried to drown you."

An interesting start...

Asher glanced over in surprise, shaken from his own thoughts. He waited a moment for wisdom to prevail, for the barrier of distance to be restored. But when it became clear the shifter was set in his course, he turned in his chair with an amused smile.

"Why, thank you."

Evie smiled in spite of herself, while Ellanden tipped the whiskey from his plate with a roll of his eyes. They'd seen people try to befriend their companion many times. Usually, such ventures ended in tears. That being said, the shifter was genuinely interested. And unnaturally determined.

And he'd been drinking for the better part of an hour.

"Is it ever strange for you?" he wondered out loud, splashing the whiskey back and forth in his glass. "Watching others partake, while you..."

He trailed off, curious but unwilling to offend.

Most people would have been offended anyway. Asher only smiled.

"It used to be," he admitted. "It isn't anymore."

Evie stared at him in silence, the smile fading from her face. She remembered the night her Uncle Aidan had brought him to the palace. Just five years old, newly orphaned, spirited away from the remains of his annihilated clan. He'd known the rules, he hadn't tried to break them, but those first few months had been hard. Hard for him and hard for the people around him. Now, the only time she even thought of him as a vampire was when she saw the fear of it in others people's eyes.

But that's not true, is it? Not after tonight...

"So you've never tried alcohol," Seth continued in the same thoughtful narrative. "You've never been high, you've never been drunk."

Asher shrugged casually, gazing out towards the fire. "I was kept in a drugged enchantment by a wizard for the better part of ten years, but I'm not sure if that counts. At any rate, I wouldn't rank it high on my list of things to repeat..."

Ellanden poured himself another drink, suppressing an involuntary shudder, while Seth stared in open fascination. Time, proximity, and alcohol had finally convinced him the vampire meant him no harm. That left him free to satisfy all those burning questions. Another few drinks and he might ask to see the fangs...

"But what if someone else has been drinking?" he pressed.

Asher shook his head, not following.

"What if you, I mean...what if the person that you..." A flicker of the fear returned as he found himself incapable of saying the rest. "...what if they'd had some?"

There was a beat of silence, then the entire table started to laugh.

"I'm not really sure." Asher tilted his head with a friendly smile. "Shall we find out?"

Seth leaned back with a shiver, deciding he didn't want to see those fangs after all. Cosette left the adoring children behind and returned to the table—flushed from the warmth of the fire. Her braids had loosened into gentle waves and a white flower was painted on her cheek.

"What are we finding out?" she asked breathlessly, a smile still lingering on her face.

"Actually, it's rather quaint," Ellanden answered with a wicked grin. "Our fearless shifter was just wondering—"

"—if you'd like another drink," Seth inserted quickly, pushing his own towards her. He lifted a finger to her cheek before lowering it with a shy smile. "They got you, too, huh?"

"What?" She blanked, then remembered the paint. "Oh—yes." She touched the paint as well, inadvertently echoing his exact words. "They're impossible to resist."

His handsome face stilled for a moment, struck by the coincidence. Ellanden sank irritably in his chair, muttering in his native tongue, "Dia ca mahret—"

Asher understood enough of the language to kick him under the table. But for once, the fae wasn't having it. Instead, he lifted his head with a rather fierce expression.

"You look well."

The accusation scorched the air between them, leaving half the table baffled and speechless while the other half deliberately avoided everyone else's eyes. The charged silence stretched on for several moments before Freya cleared her throat loudly and lifted the flagon once more.

"I think that calls for another round..."

THE WHISKEY DID THE trick, cooling tempers and smoothing over arguments that would be better left until tomorrow. Under its coaxing hand, the friends forgot about the troubles plaguing them and allowed themselves to do something they hadn't done in an awfully long time.

Act their age.

"There were seventeen."

"There were five."

"There were seventeen."

"There were *five*."

"Asher, you're forgetting—"

"Ellanden, there were *five* men stationed outside the throne room. Any numbers added onto that are just an egotistical inflation of your own imagination."

"Yes, but you're *forgetting* the twelve soldiers who were sleeping in the antechamber," the prince insisted. "I pity your abysmal storytelling, so we'll chalk it up to a temporary lapse in pride."

The vampire chuckled, fluttering his fingers in the flame of a candle.

"So as I was saying," the fae cleared his throat, "there were seventeen—"

"You're all mad," Seth murmured. It was the first time he'd spoken in several minutes and the rest of the friends turned to him in surprise. He lifted his eyes over the sea of empty goblets to the intoxicated prince and the vampire sitting by his side. "I saw you massacre half a beach of Carpathian soldiers. And you—you sank a pair of warships with a flaming arrow. How is it possible that either of you cares how many guards you bested in some stupid castle. Why does it matter?"

The rest of them flushed, but the prince regarded him coldly.

"It matters because I was six. And it wasn't a castle," he added under his breath, "it was a palace—there's a difference. You'd know that if you hadn't been raised in a barn."

Evie kicked him sharply beneath the table. "What did we say about saying things like that?"

"Say them quieter—"

"Keep them to yourself."

The others continued talking, oblivious to the exchange.

In the clearing around them, the party raged on. Most of the children had been put to bed, and people who remained were under the heavy influence of a feast's worth of alcohol. The empty bottles were kicked discreetly under the table. More bottles were being opened and poured.

"—not like you would have gotten into trouble anyway," Cosette was saying, resting her chin on the table while absentmindedly playing with a knife. "What was your father going to do, banish you for stealing his crown? It's not like any of those guards was actually going to hurt you—"

"Wait," Seth interrupted, fighting back a smile, "you stole from your own father? That's the big accomplishment? Stealing your dad's crown?"

"To start," Ellanden answered sharply, "it wasn't my father's and it wasn't a crown. It was the royal scepter of Belaria. And I was planning on returning it right after I'd decapitated the agreed upon statue. I just happened to drop it accidentally in the courtyard pond."

The others stared in silence and he lifted his glass with a shrug.

"It was a dare."

Seth shook his head incredulously. "Who in their right mind would dare you to such a thing?"

Evie raised her hand in silence.

"You're all mad," the shifter said again, this time with the hint of a smile. His eyes lifted to Cosette, twinkling in the light of the fire. "These are the games you played growing up?"

She shook her head practically, dissecting a slice of mango with her knife. "I was just a child. Most of the games I played involved me imagining I was a pony."

There was a pause.

"Imagining you *had* a pony."

"I'm afraid not."

The shifter laughed as a sudden cheer rose up from the other side of the bonfire. A group of teenage witches was taking turns attempting to harness the flames. The one who finally managed it got cocky, raising her arms in triumph...and subsequently lighting her skirt on fire.

Holy crap—

Evie half-pushed to her feet, watching as the witch's friends doused her in water, laughing when she began cursing in some foreign tongue. Whatever limited inhibitions the village maintained had vanished amidst the haze of whiskey, and things were getting heated as the night wore on.

Shifters were slinking into the shadows with witches. A pair of warlocks was glued at the mouth. At some unseen signal the fiddlers picked up the pace and a swarm of people flooded towards the grass by the fire, their bodies glistening with sweat as they danced in front of the flames.

"This must be why they don't really wear clothes," Freya remarked casually, watching as two shifters tangled themselves together. "Saves them the trouble of having to take them off—"

No sooner had she spoken than there was a tap on her shoulder. The friends looked up to see a teenage wolf standing in the darkness with a smile. He looked the witch up and down before cocking his head towards the fire. "Care for a dance?"

...or something like it.

Freya froze in surprise, caught completely off guard. She hadn't noticed him, but the man had apparently been watching her for quite some time. And he had a lot more than dancing on his mind. Her lips parted, but before she could answer Ellanden dismissed him with a wave of his glass.

"She's taken."

The others turned to him at the same time, fighting back smiles as he poured himself another drink. When he saw them watching, he lifted a shoulder in a careless shrug.

"Best not to split up. We still don't know what these people want."

Asher's eyes twinkled with a secret smile. "I think they made it very clear what they want."

The fae purposely ignored him, while the others made an effort not to laugh. The only one who looked secretly pleased was Freya, though for once she was keeping her opinion to herself.

It might have been the first proposition, but it was in no way the last.

As the night wore on, the villagers—who at first had kept a careful distance—grew more and more bold, making their way in shifts towards the table in an attempt to engage the beautiful travelers dining in their midst. The two princesses were asked to dance enough times that the men eventually made it into a drinking game. Ellanden received just as many offers, all of which he politely declined, and Seth was invited to take a midnight walk with a witch who looked about ready to set him on fire if he refused. He refused anyway, watching nervously as she made her way back to the rest of her coven, a little trail of sparks dripping from her hands.

"You should have gone," Asher teased quietly. "She probably hexed your drink."

The vampire was the only one who hadn't been propositioned over the course of the evening. There had been plenty of stares, plenty of whispered conversations, but no one could seem to get past the fangs.

Instead of being offended he was greatly enjoying himself, offering a hilarious running commentary as his friends stammered and flailed with each drunken attempt.

Seth stifled a shudder, glancing down at his glass. "Don't say that..."

The vampire leaned forward with mock concern, also examining the goblet. "Sprinkle in some grass...that's how you can know for sure."

In a moment of pure intoxication, the shifter actually glanced beneath the table. Then he set the glass down slowly, regarding the vampire with a rueful smile.

"It's easy for you...no one dares to come close."

Asher's smile faltered for a second, then he turned back to the fire. "That's true."

No one else noticed. The rest of them were focused on the party and their drink. But the princess froze where she sat, feeling suddenly cold. Her eyes travelled across the table, but Asher wasn't looking at her. He wasn't really looking at anything. But his eyes were fixed on the people dancing by the fire, like there was some kind of wall between them. One he could never breach.

"—don't know what you're talking about," Ellanden was saying, winking at a nymph who was staring at him across the grass. "They're not all so bad."

Evie shook herself back to the present, swallowing the lump that had risen in her throat. It was easier to do with whiskey. Though not everyone had such a luxury.

The others were still talking, but much to Ellanden's embarrassment the nymph had taken the wink as an invitation and was heading their way. He flushed ever so slightly at the presence of his friends, but straightened up with a charming smile. A smile that faded almost immediately...

...as the nymph melted into the shape of a man.

"Eli?!"

STRENGTH

The princess couldn't help but gasp aloud. The rest of them were staring in utter disbelief, but none so much as Ellanden who literally whitened with rage.

"What the heck is wrong with you!"

The shape-shifter merely laughed, pulling up a chair next to Evie. "Relax, I was just having a bit of fun." He poured himself a glass of ale, though it was clear he'd had plenty, before stretching his legs with a self-satisfied smirk. "Besides, wasn't it *you* who beckoned *me*?"

The fae's eyes narrowed in a vengeful glare, but now that the shock had worn off the rest of the friends found the prank downright hilarious. They pulled their chairs closer, gathering in delight.

"You're a shape-shifter?" Freya asked in astonishment, forgetting, for a drunken moment, the true identity of the people who sat beside her. "I've never met one before."

Asher silently confiscated her whiskey, while Cosette shook her head with a sigh.

"At your service," Eli answered with a grin, casting a sideways look at Evie. "And I'm not surprised you've never met one. My particular brand of magic is exceedingly rare."

The friends shared a secret grin, thinking the same thing.

Ellanden's ego cannot take this.

Sure enough, Ellanden was staring deliberately at the table—taking measured breaths while carefully pouring himself a glass of ale. The shape-shifter was oblivious. As was the witch.

"So can you turn into anyone?" Freya gushed. "Anyone at all?"

Eli flashed her a quick smile before returning his eyes to the princess.

"I can be anyone you want me to be..."

Asher glanced up sharply, while Seth leaned forward with a grin.

"But it must be really hard, right?" he asked innocently. "Taking someone else's shape? I would imagine only a handful of people in the realm could possibly manage it."

Eli nodded importantly, while Ellanden silently drained his glass.

"It's harder than you can possibly imagine," the shape-shifter replied.

Cosette nodded thoughtfully, eyes wide as saucers.

"It says a lot about you as a person," she murmured. "To have been chosen by the fates for that sort of thing."

The glass shattered in Ellanden's hand. He wiped it discreetly beneath the table.

"That's what they say," Eli answered smugly, leaning back in his chair. "There's a reason the Kreo traditionally chose us shape-shifters to lead the tribe—"

There was a sharp burst of laughter, and the entire table turned to the fae. He had been trying extremely hard to contain himself, but some offenses were too great to ignore.

"And you're leading this tribe, are you?" he asked sarcastically. "The old man who greeted us and called himself chief...that was more of an honorary title?"

Eli's eyes narrowed in dislike. "I'm not saying I'm the chief. I'm just—"

"You're just what?" the fae interrupted.

There was a charged pause.

"Forget it," Eli scoffed. "You wouldn't understand."

The prince's hands balled into fists.

"*I* wouldn't get it—" He caught himself suddenly, looking past the shifter to where the rest of his friends were watching with silent amusement. A look of intense frustration flashed across his face before he leaned back suddenly in his chair. "You're right—I wouldn't get it."

Evie bit her lip to keep from laughing. Even Asher couldn't help but smile.

It was probably the farthest the fae had ever stretched his patience, but the stars were aligned against him and he couldn't get a break. Instead of changing the subject the shape-shifter zeroed in with unnatural precision, leaning forward to examine him for the first time.

"Actually, we had a prince once who was part fae," he said conversationally.

Ellanden looked away quickly, wishing he could also change his face, while Seth cocked his head with an innocent smile. "You don't say..."

Eli laughed shortly, taking a drink from his cup.

"The guy was a bit of a legend. Not because of his magic—he never cared for anything like that." He lifted his eyes to the drunken festivities. "But because of nights like this."

The friends turned to him with sudden interest, leaning forward at the same time.

Since they were children, Ellanden had been loath to talk about the time he spent amongst his mother's people. But over the years, little things had slipped out. Spells he'd heard, people he'd met. Evie knew for a fact that he'd lost his virginity in a place like this, although the circumstances under which it happened had never been made clear.

"Really," she said with a coaxing smile, "do tell..."

The shape-shifter opened his mouth to reply, but Ellanden beat him to it.

"That's not...I mean...we don't have to..." He trailed off in dismay, staring back at five uncompromising smiles. "It's unseemly to discuss such things—"

"The guy's dead," Eli interrupted callously. "What does it matter?"

The smiles faded. Even Seth lost his humor. The only one who didn't notice was the shape-shifter himself. He leaned back instead, sipping whiskey and preaching to a captive audience.

"We don't have many fae," he continued casually, "the guy's father married into it, so he was a bit of a novelty. Lots of great stories to choose from, but the best is probably the day it all started."

Ellanden paled in horror, but there was nothing to be done.

"The day it all started?" Asher prompted with a curious frown. "What do you mean?"

"The guy's birthday," Eli clarified, downing the rest like a shot. "Once he turned fourteen, the rest of the tribe decided he was fair game. Made quite the show of welcoming him to the fold."

Evie lifted her eyebrows ever so slightly, glancing at Ellanden. From everything she knew about him—and she knew a lot—she would bet that he hadn't exactly shied away from the attention.

Not like he was doing now.

"I'm serious." He glanced around the clearing, pulling at the neck of his tunic like it was suddenly hard to breathe. "Can't we just—"

"Seems there was a whole group of people lining up to deflower the prince," Eli concluded with a smile. "Literally *lining up* outside his chamber, waiting their turn. Accounts vary as to how many there actually were, but if you believe the rumors he was more than happy to oblige."

A hushed silence fell over the table.

Then everyone turned to the fae at the same time.

"Are you serious?"

"I believe the rumors."

"Over-compensating for something..."

"It's a miracle he didn't come away with some kind of disease."

"That's enough, all right?" Ellanden interrupted them, trying to maintain what was left of his dignity. "We don't know the whole story...maybe he was lonely."

Seth pursed his lips. "Doesn't sound like it..."

The fae shot him an icy look. "Maybe he was *lonely* because, while he'd been exiled to the jungle, the rest of his friends got a summer of sparring at the palace. Maybe he was coping the only way he knew how."

The vampire laughed under his breath, while Evie folded her arms with a sarcastic grin.

"Oh—*that's* what it was? He was self-medicating?"

Ellanden's eyes flashed but he glanced at Eli and visibly reined himself in, biting back his retort and answering with a mild, "...one might suppose."

The entire table erupted in laughter, forgetting themselves completely as it went on loud and long. The only people who didn't partake were Eli—who didn't know why it was happening, and Freya—who didn't find it as funny as all the rest. And of course Ellanden himself—who silently vowed to murder each and every one of them before the night was through.

It was still going on when the chief stood up suddenly, silencing the party with a single gesture as he turned towards his guests with a raised glass.

"To the tides...washing up new friends on our humble shores."

The friends blushed and smiled as the eyes of the entire village turned their way. How kind of him to include the shipwreck, but the Kreo were a blunt people, and their chief didn't stop there.

"We're sorry for our initial welcome. I'm told things got off to a rocky start..." As if the rest of them didn't know what he meant, he was quick to clarify. "We tried to drown the vampire."

There was a tittering of nervous laughter—laughter that got louder as time went on.

Asher shook his head in exasperation, but it was so charmingly said even he couldn't help but smile. Some of the witches who'd taken part actually lifted their hands in an apologetic wave, while the warlock who'd orchestrated the whole thing gave a careless shrug.

The chief's eyes twinkled before growing suddenly thoughtful.

"Whatever path has brought you, we are glad for your arrival. Whatever time you spend, we pray it treats you well. And whatever day you choose to leave us, we hope the tides will bring you back again. But for now, drink and be merry. For the night is young..."

The rest of the tribe chanted along.

"...and we'll soon return to the stars."

Ellanden mouthed the words along with the rest of them, unable to resist a tiny smile. The friends lifted their glasses and drank deeply, every one of them taking the words to heart. There was no telling what the future might hold, but for now they were content to live in the present.

For however long they could make it last...

Chapter 11

There were few things more inviting after a long night than the sight of an empty bed.

Evie had sunk into hers without thinking, without undressing, without doing anything more than trying to kick off her shoes. At that point, she remembered she wasn't wearing any. At that point, she remembered she was basically undressed already. At that point, she promptly blacked out.

When she pried open her eyes the next morning, shafts of filtered sunlight were already pouring into the room. It took a few seconds to remember what had happened, to remember where she was. Not only in a Kreo camp but in a glorified tree fort, seeing that sunlight from fifty feet up.

She rolled over slowly, blinking in silence out the open window.

Things hadn't died down after the chief's toast. If anything, the party had only picked up speed. The older members of the village had gone to bed, leaving the younger members free to do as they wished. There were sparring matches and more dancing. Forgotten fights and fits of laughter. Whatever bottles of whiskey and ale that hadn't already been consumed were unearthed from some back-up location and carried in triumph to the tables. After that, memories started to blur...

Evie remembered Eli asking her to dance. Seth and Cosette were already tangled together by the fire, lost in their own world. She remembered meeting Asher's eyes across the table, remembered the exact look on his face. Then things took a turn for the worse.

Ellanden said something rude. Freya attempted a drunken spell. The table went flying and its occupants scattered. There was a chance the princess had fallen into the mud...?

She pulled back the blanket, glancing down at her bare feet.

Sure enough, there were little streaks of dirt and grass laced around her ankles, along with something that looked suspiciously like paint. She reached out a hand to examine it, only to see that there was paint on her arms as well. A rather crude design. She was horrified she'd done it herself.

"Morning."

She lifted her head to see Ellanden standing in the doorway, looking like a slightly hungover angel, gripping two steaming cups and staring down at her with a sunlit smile.

The feast had left a lasting impression on him as well. In addition to the swirling designs painted on his skin, the fae had apparently embraced the Kreo dress code. Instead of his usual tunic and cloak, he was wearing the same leather bands as the rest of them. They clung to his fair skin like they'd been painted as well, curving around each muscle and hanging loose on his hips.

A far cry from his usual refinement. But the strange thing was, it oddly suited him.

Evie took the cup, patting the bed beside her. "You've embraced the wardrobe, I see."

He settled down beside her, glancing at himself a bit self-consciously. "You like?"

She nodded faintly, lifting a finger to trace the leather bands on his chest. They ran from shoulder to hip—stretching across him in a giant X. Between that, the braided hair, and the swirls of henna, it was a side of him she'd never seen before. One she'd never even considered.

"You look like a jungle mercenary," she said practically. "It's quite fetching."

He laughed and finished the rest of his drink. "Excellent."

The princess was supposed to be sharing a room with the rest of the girls, but they were nowhere in sight. Judging from the position of the sun, it was already coming on noon. They'd probably left ages ago. Either that, or they'd never made it back for the night.

She thought again of Seth and Cosette, rotating slowly in front of the fire. It looked like the shifter's plan had skipped a couple phases and gone right to the end.

"That was a crazy party," she murmured, inhaling a breath of sweet-smelling steam. She took a tentative sip and smiled, tasting flowers and honey. "I think we decimated their alcohol supply."

Ellanden shrugged, gazing at the paint swirled across her body.

"They can always get more. At any rate, it's why I wanted to check on you." He flashed another blinding smile. "That was a small ocean of whiskey you drank last night."

Seven hells...you're right.

As if on cue, the image brightened unbearably and the throbbing of a migraine began pounding the inside of her brain. She lifted a hand with a grimace, cursing under her breath.

"I'd like to say it was worth it but, to be honest, I don't really remember."

They laughed quietly and he pressed the cup back into her hand.

"Drink up—it'll help."

She took another long sip, staring out the window as he began playing absentmindedly with her hair. She might not remember the feast itself, but she was painfully aware of what had happened before in Asher's room. A sudden chill swept over her as she played back each moment with perfect clarity—crushed beneath him on the mattress, her bare legs encircling his waist.

It could have been perfect. It *should* have been perfect.

But then there was the blood.

Her face stilled as she remembered it—the way it had looked, dripping down his skin. Never had she been more truly aware of what he was than in that very moment. Suddenly, it was easy to understand the way other people looked at him. Suddenly, it was easy to understand the fear.

A vampire was a predator.

And she'd invited one into her bed—

"What's the matter?" Ellanden asked softly. She startled in surprise, and he brushed back a lock of her hair with a gentle smile. "You're a thousand miles away."

She blushed and dropped her eyes to the blanket, lightly kicking it off her legs. "Just trying to remember what happened last night," she said evasively, gesturing to the swirls of henna looping across her thighs. "I might have attempted an art project."

He laughed again, running the tip of his finger along her ribcage. There was henna there, too, swirling in an uneven pattern down her sides. "I think it turned out okay..."

She shivered a little under his touch, then turned to face him.

"Ellanden...do you think we should ask the chief about the shipwreck?"

He pulled back a few inches, staring with a frown. "What do you mean? Why would he know anything about it?"

"Do you remember what you told me back in Belaria, about the Kreo having certain elixirs and spells that can help you remember things once forgotten?"

He froze a second, then nodded quickly.

"So maybe he would have something to help me remember the shipwreck."

The fae stared another moment, then shook his head. "Why would you want to?"

In all fairness, it was a good question. She remembered enough of the moments beforehand to know that she wasn't going to like what was coming next. But she couldn't shake the feeling that something didn't add up. That they were missing some crucial piece of the puzzle.

Then there are my dreams...

"It's just...unsettling," she deflected again, setting her cup on the floor. "I can't remember anything after being thrown into the water, and you said yourself that you had no idea how we could have washed up on such a distant shore. We're missing something. And I need to know what it is."

He nodded distractedly, trailing a finger down the side of her arm.

"*Landi.*"

He blinked quickly, dropping his hand.

"Sorry—what?"

She looked him over with a frown, clearly underestimating his own hangover.

"The chief," she repeated. "Do you think he could help me with something like that?"

He lowered his eyes quickly, staring into his lap. "Yeah, uh...that's a good idea."

She frowned again, leaning down to catch his gaze. "Are you okay? You're acting weird."

He sat there a moment, then shook his head with a sigh.

"Not really," he said quietly. "I guess...I must remember more of the shipwreck than you."

Her lips parted in surprise.

"But you said that you didn't," she murmured. "In the cart on the way over here, you said that you could only remember fragments—"

"That's true," he said quickly, "but it's been coming back to me. Like pieces of a dream."

She scooted instinctively closer, reaching out to take his hand.

"Tell me..."

It was quiet for a few moments as the fae stared at the bedcover, deep in thought. Without seeming to think about it, he closed his hand gently—lacing his fingers through hers.

"It's feelings more than memories," he finally confessed. "The shock of being thrown into the water, the panic watching the ship sink into the waves." A shiver ran down his arms. "I couldn't think, I couldn't breathe...I was terrified."

Evie's heart broke a thousand times over. In all the years they'd known each other, she could count on one hand the number of times the fae had shown such emotion. As if his quiet words weren't enough, the look on his face was breaking her heart.

"I felt the same way," she murmured, rubbing soothing circles on his back. "And without being able to remember, I keep feeling like part of me is still back there. Like it hasn't finished yet."

He lifted his eyes, staring vacantly into the trees.

"I remember," he said softly. "I remember seeing the mast crack in half, watching the anchor drag it down into the sea. I remember seeing you in the water above me," he continued suddenly, "floating in the waves with your eyes closed."

A strange look came over his face as he turned towards her. His fingers tightened with a belated rush of emotion as his other hand slipped behind her hair.

"I didn't think I was ever going to see you again."

Their eyes met...then he was kissing her.

What the—?!

Her eyes shot open as his lips brushed against her mouth. A muted cry rose up in her throat, but it was like a shockwave had exploded in her brain. Words failed her. Thought failed her.

She was simply stunned.

Quick as it started, the kiss immediately deepened. His fingers curled into her hair, and he was easing her down onto the bed. His body, which she knew so well, felt suddenly unfamiliar, flushed with heat and stretching out on top of hers. Those radiant eyes were closed as he pulled her even closer, his hand was sliding up her skirt—

"ARE YOU CRAZY?!"

She smacked him upside the head, wrenching herself free. He sprang back, pale as a sheet, but she wasn't finished. Before he could recover his balance, she shoved him right off the bed.

The door opened as she shouted again.

STRENGTH 139

"ARE YOU STILL DRUNK?!"

But that's when everything got very strange.

Because that's when she looked up and saw Asher and Ellanden standing at the door.

It was impossible to say who looked more surprised, the vampire or the princess. Truth be told, it was probably the fae. His lips parted in astonishment as he stared down at himself, lying on the floor. The room was quiet for a moment, then the air shimmered and Eli appeared in his place.

"*You*!" Evie gasped, both fists still raised in the air.

The fae shook his head slowly, utterly bewildered by what he'd just seen.

"What the hell were you doing..."

The shape-shifter was panting, but there was something triumphant about his expression as he pushed slowly to his feet. He returned the fae's question with a smug smile.

"Making out with your girlfriend."

There was a beat of silence.

Followed by another.

Ellanden's eyebrows lifted, but he was too surprised to make any other reaction. He simply shook his head, correcting the shifter's mistake.

"She's not my girlfriend."

Eli's grin faded slightly before vanishing clean away.

"...she's not?"

The fae pointed to the vampire.

"She's *his* girlfriend."

A chilling silence descended over the room.

The princess was seething. The vampire was dangerously quiet. The shape-shifter looked like he was on the verge of throwing up. Only the fae was starting to find the humor.

"Guess that almighty gift of yours comes with a few drawbacks...judgement being one."

Eli quickly backed up to the wall, grabbing his empty cup as if some strange compulsion had prompted him not to leave behind a mess.

"I'm just going to go..." he muttered.

Since the men were standing in front of the door he swiftly made his way to the window—jumping out without a moment's pause. For a split second the princess forgot to be angry and scrambled across the bed, half-expecting to see him splattered fifty feet beneath them on the ground.

He wasn't. He wasn't anywhere in sight. *That* crisis was temporarily handled.

Another was just getting warmed up.

The fae got things started by making them worse.

"How was it?" he asked brightly.

Evie's eyes snapped shut, trying to bleach the image from her mind.

"I can't even look at you," she muttered.

He ignored this, cocking his head with a smirk. "I bet it was good, right?"

"Can you give us a minute?" Asher interrupted softly.

The humor abruptly vanished, leaving a sudden chill in its wake. The fae's smile faded as he nodded quickly, backing towards the door. It was already open. He glanced once more between his friends, lips parting with some uncertain thought before he reconsidered and left them alone, shutting the door quietly behind him.

For what felt like an eternity, neither was able to speak. When it got to be too much Asher finally cleared his throat, glancing towards the window where Eli had escaped.

"Did he try to—"

"No," she said quickly. "No, it was just a stupid prank. I'll kill him for it soon enough."

From the look on the vampire's face, he clearly intended to beat her to the punch. But he said nothing. He merely stood in silence, staring at the floor.

"Why are you here?" Evie finally asked. When he looked up with a question she rephrased it, trying to steady her shaking voice. "You wanted a minute to talk?"

He stared a second longer then nodded quickly, trying to refocus his thoughts. It took a few moments, and when he finally did speak it was the last thing she expected him to say.

"What do you remember about last night?'

Her face lightened in surprise.

"Last night?" Her mind blanked, fighting through the drunken stupor. "Not much...why?"

A strange look swept over him, but his eyes were glued to the floor.

"Ellanden and Seth were arguing over some nonsense," he said in a quiet monotone. "Freya tried to cast a spell to break them apart. The table flipped and you were thrown backwards."

He froze perfectly still.

"And when I reached out to catch you...you started to cry."

She stared back in shock, unable to believe it was true. But even as he said the words, she started to remember. The wave of fear that swept over her. The haunted look on his face.

"I wasn't..." She trailed off, uncertain how to finish. "That was just—"

"I'm sorry about earlier," he said quietly. "In my room."

Another rip in the fabric. Another crack in the stone.

"Asher," she said with a hint of desperation, "just stop it, okay? I was *drunk*. I didn't know what I was doing. And before—"

"Before?" he said softly. "When I tried to have sex with you while drinking your blood?"

A ringing silence fell between them.

He looked at her for the first time.

"I never understood it before, but I do now. There's a reason why people like you and me don't get together. There's a reason why a shifter and a vampire could never fall in love."

A pair of tears slipped down her face, gone before she could stop them.

"Ash, that's not...that's not true."

He smiled sadly. At least he tried. Something had died inside him the moment he saw the princess' tears. A part of him wasn't sure he'd ever smile again.

"It *is* true," he murmured. "Even if I wish it wasn't. Even if I would give everything I had just to—" He caught himself quickly, backing towards the door. "We were kidding ourselves."

He slipped outside with that same heartbreaking smile.

"It was never going to be me."

Chapter 12

The princess sat by herself at the edge of a meadow, staring in silence across the grass.

Considering how few hours she'd been awake, the day was already unsalvageable. The henna smeared across her body refused to come off, the miracle hangover cure she'd been promised wasn't working, and the man she was falling in love with had just told her such love was impossible.

Then he'd walked away.

He broke up with me. He actually broke up with me.

A part of her still couldn't believe it. She'd sat on the bed for a full hour, staring blankly at the door, just waiting for him to come back. When that hadn't happened she'd cried a little, tried her luck with the henna, then wandered to the edge of the jungle encampment—arms hanging limp by her sides, the hem of her clumsily-tied cloak trailing miserably on the ground.

Strangely enough, it was the logistics that concerned her. She simply didn't know what she was going to do next. Who would she joke with? Who would she think about? Who would share the other half of her blanket when the friends stretched out to sleep beneath the stars?

So much of her time had been spent dedicated to this one man. Now that he'd removed himself from the picture, she wasn't quite sure how the rest of it fit.

The sound of distant laughter lifted her eyes.

The children who'd been dancing in front of the fire were playing in the meadow now, and they certainly weren't playing alone. She watched with a soft smile as Ellanden abandoned all dignity to frolic beside them, scooping them off the ground and tossing them high into the air.

At least someone's having a good day.

Fae were openly affectionate with children. Playing with them, singing to them, kissing their cheeks when they cried. To be a child in the land of Fae was to be something treasured.

Growing up in the palace, it was the only time she saw her Uncle Cassiel be silly. There was no limit to the things he would do. Reading them stories, putting on voices, chasing them around the gardens like a lion and thrashing them with his teeth. It was a side of him revealed only in their presence. *And* her father's. That playfulness was one of the things only Dylan could bring out in him. Coincidentally, it was one of the reasons the Fae Council hated the King of Belaria so much.

"All right, who's next?"

She glanced up again to see the prince literally dripping in children. They were hanging from his arms, from his hands, from his neck. A few had even grabbed onto his ankles. All were shrieking with such breathless laughter it was a miracle none of them had passed out.

Most people would have surrendered. The fae was just getting warmed up.

She smiled again, forcing herself to clear the darkness and think on something good.

His father had been the same way. Endlessly patient. Endlessly energetic. Some days he'd carry the sleeping children back in his arms, having tired them into a night of blissful dreams.

A witch appeared at the edge of the clearing—shouting something and waving what looked like a soup ladle over her head. The children scattered immediately, doubling back only to wish the fae a breathless goodbye. One of the smallest ones, a girl of no more than five, actually grabbed his hand, tugging him down far enough that she could press a quick kiss to his cheek.

He stared after them with a smile, windswept and disheveled. Then he saw Evie watching and lifted a hand in surprise. He headed over a moment later, cutting gracefully through the grass.

"Don't your arms get tired?" she greeted him, wiping her cheeks quickly before he could see any evidence of tears. "You must have thrown the entire village."

He let out a sparkling laugh, stretching out beside her. "Tired? You insult me."

She smiled humorlessly, staring out towards the trees. "Yeah, I've apparently been doing a lot of that lately..."

They sat there a while longer, staring at the horizon in contented silence. Then she glanced over suddenly and yanked a lock of his messy hair.

"Everly!" he cried, shoving her hand away. "You're lucky I don't have my knife."

She let out a quiet laugh, turning back towards the trees. "Yep—that's the real you."

He stared a moment in confusion, then his face relaxed with a smile. A second later, he was chuckling as well—remembering their unconventional meeting earlier that morning.

"How could you think that was me?" he chided. "Kissing you? I mean—no offense, Evie, but...*kissing* you?"

She smacked him with a grin. "How could I *not* take offense at that?"

"And the things he said," Ellanden continued, making his voice theatrically aloof as he quoted the lines, "I remember going into the water..." She chortled in spite of herself and he shook his head with a grin. "It was a shipwreck, not a play."

She giggled again, then stopped just as quick. "Wait—how do you know what he said to me?"

Ellanden's eyes flashed, and for a second he looked abruptly dangerous. "I asked him."

...were there weapons involved?

Normally, she would have asked. Normally, she would have cared. But the shifter deserved whatever was coming to him. She was just surprised the fae had gotten to him first.

And on that note...

"Asher and I broke up," she announced suddenly.

Ellanden turned to her in shock.

"Because of the kiss?" he asked incredulously. "Evie, that wasn't your fault—"

"Not because of the kiss," she interrupted, keeping her eyes on the trees. "There were other things that...it wasn't because of the kiss."

He wanted to ask, but didn't. He kept quiet instead. After a few painful moments he shot her a secret look, then wrapped an arm around her trembling shoulders.

A pair of tears slipped down her face. She wiped them quickly with the back of her hand.

"Now's your time to gloat," she said, forcing another smile. "We broke up, just like you wanted. Couldn't even make it a few weeks—"

He shook his head, giving her shoulders a gentle squeeze. "Believe what you like, but I honestly didn't want that."

No, you didn't. Neither did I.

Part of the logistics the princess was having such trouble with was the breakup itself. Seeing as she'd never really dated anyone, she had nothing to compare it to. She liked to think that she was keeping it together. She liked to think she was handling it well. If handling it well implied wandering to the edge of a jungle and debating whether she was ever going to come back...

"You wouldn't understand," she teased, wiping away more tears. "They couldn't get enough of you. I heard people were *lining up* just for the chance."

His face stilled for a moment, then he dropped his arm with a blush. "Yeah, that...that isn't exactly what happened."

She stared at him questioningly and he let out a quiet sigh.

"It was my birthday and people were lining up…just not for that."

She shook her head in confusion. "For what, then?"

He debated refusing, then decided her plight was more urgent than his own. "The Kreo have this blessing—they use it on strangers and people who've returned after having been a long time away. They gave me the blessing, kissed my cheek…then left."

Her eyebrows lifted in astonishment. "So how did the rumor get started?"

He shrugged. "Someone probably saw it from a distance and drew their own conclusions about what was happening."

Her lips curved in a genuine smile. "And you didn't bother correcting them."

He flashed her a quick grin. "It must have slipped my mind."

She laughed again, leaning against him as the tears continued pouring down her face. It seemed no matter what she did, she couldn't stop them. They came and went as they pleased.

"Asher and I…we started… things got pretty, uh, intense."

The fae stiffened, but didn't say anything. He simply nodded, waiting for the rest.

"Except, when the moment came…"

She broke off with a shiver, remembering it all with perfect clarity.

Never had she been so happy. Never had she wanted something so badly. She loved Asher. She trusted him completely. She was ready to do this with him. She'd been ready for a long time.

Then she saw the blood on his face…and her entire body went cold.

"I was afraid of him," she finished quietly.

Ellanden looked over suddenly, then reached out to take her hand. "It was your first time," he said softly. "It's only natural to be—"

"I wasn't afraid of that," she interrupted, staring down at their fingers. "I was afraid of *him*."

The fae stared at her a moment before dropping his gaze to the grass. An intense expression was warring just behind them. The desire to help the tear-stained girl beside him, and the silent vow he'd made to keep some secrets forever to himself.

Fae were notoriously proud...but also shockingly selfless.

"After what happened in the mine," he began quietly, "I was afraid of Asher."

The princess looked up suddenly, surprised to hear him admit such a thing.

"Of course you were," she said after a moment. "He was about to *kill* you, Ellanden. You would have been certifiable not to have been afraid—"

"*After*," the fae interrupted. "I was afraid of him *after*."

She stared at him in silence. He stared at his hands.

"We've spent every single moment together since it happened. There's just never been a chance to..." He trailed off, shaking his head. "Those first few days, I couldn't tear my eyes away from him. I was always watching, always knew where he was. Those first few nights...I couldn't stop thinking of it. I'd just lie there, pretending to sleep, playing it over again and again."

The wind picked up around them and he pulled in a breath.

"He's a vampire, Everly. A part of us is right to be afraid." He turned to look at her. "But that doesn't change what we know to be true."

She stared at him miserably, eyes blurring with tears. "And what's that?"

He softened with a gentle smile, wiping them from her face. "That he's *our* vampire. A friend we've loved since childhood. A part of our family." He knocked his forehead lightly against hers. "Even if he scares us every now and again..."

She warmed in spite of herself. Her lips curved with the beginning of a smile. But it died as quickly as it started, leaving her numb and cold.

"That might be true, but it doesn't matter." She pulled in a quick breath, turning her eyes back to the trees. "I didn't break up with Asher. He broke up with me."

A flash of anger swept across the prince's face, but he controlled it quickly. The stick he'd been playing with wasn't so lucky, shattering in his fingers before crumbling to dust. After a few seconds of measured breathing, he glanced down at her once more.

"He broke up with—"

"There you are! We've been looking everywhere for you!"

The friends looked up quickly as Seth and Freya appeared at the far edge of the field. Both had apparently recovered from the night's festivities and were wearing their own clothes. They lifted their hands in a simultaneous wave and started heading across the grass.

Evie wiped her cheeks. Ellanden dusted the pieces of stick from his hands. They had just pushed to their feet, when she grabbed him suddenly; lowering her voice with a last minute request.

"Please don't say anything," she pleaded. "And don't be angry with Asher. I told you because I needed a friend. I don't want you to take sides."

Judging by the look on the fae's face, a great deal of that was already out of her control. But he nodded quickly, gave her a kiss on the cheek, then turned around with a welcoming smile.

"Good morning."

"Good *afternoon*," Freya corrected. "What are you guys doing out here? The rest of the village already gathered for lunch."

The pair shared a quick look, then Ellanden shrugged it off with a distracting smile.

"We decided to go on without you," he announced. "Evie and I are the only useful members of this quest. The rest of you are dead weight."

Seth snorted with laughter, while Freya shook her head.

"Don't let the vampire hear you say that."

Ellanden tensed ever so slightly before smoothing his face clear.

"Three shall set out, though three shall not return...?" He let the words hang for a moment before shrugging them off with another smile. "We've decided Asher will be the one to die.

So much for not taking sides...

"You know, I'm surprised the chief didn't recognize Asher," Seth said suddenly. "After that speech he gave about having met 'one civilized vampire'. He clearly knew the guy's father."

Evie tried not to flinch. Her chest tightened every time she heard the name.

"Then Asher must not have been with him," Ellanden said quickly, continuing to speak for the both of them. "Aidan's been trying to unite the vampire factions for decades, since long before any of us was born. The chief looks about a thousand. They could have met each other any time."

"That's fascinating," Freya muttered. When the rest of them turned to her, she pointed back to the village. "*Lunch*. I'm starving here. And I need something to counteract the whiskey..."

Ellanden glanced down at her sympathetically. "They make this flowery kind of tea—"

"It doesn't work," Seth and Evie said at the same time.

The witch pointed to the camp once more, this time firing out an unintentional burst of sparks. Seth chuckled and headed after her, but when Evie tied to follow she was pulled back.

"Go on without us," Ellanden called, holding on to her shoulder. "We'll catch up."

The others vanished into the trees, throwing curious glances over their shoulders. The princess was curious as well, but before she could ask the fae caught her in an enormous hug.

"What—"

She broke off with a suffocated gasp. A second later, she buried her face in his cloak.

She hadn't realized how much she needed to be held until that very moment. She hadn't even realized she was still trembling until his arms circled around her, keeping her still.

"I just can't believe it," she whispered. "I can't believe it—"

He squeezed tighter, kissing the top of her head. "I know."

They held each other another minute, then he pulled back—brushing the tears from her face. He finished with a sympathetic grimace, flicking the bottom of her chin.

"You know...you kind of have to shelf this. Just until we save the world."

She let out a burst of laughter, bowing her head.

"Yeah, I figured." She took another second to get herself together then looked up at him suddenly, squinting in the afternoon sun. "Thanks, Landi."

He answered with a smile, steering her gently across the field.

"You need food," he declared. "It's the only way to get through a break-up."

She shook her head with a faint grin. "How would you know? Has anyone ever broken up with you before?"

He thought about it for a moment. "A woman I was seeing once felt compelled to return to the sea."

She shot him a quick look, then kept walking.

"I'm not sure if that counts..."

BY THE TIME EVIE AND Ellanden cleared the last of the trees and entered the village, the noon-time feast was mostly finished. The tables had been scraped and cleared, with only a few hungover stragglers staggering in from the tree-fort, scrounging around for what was left.

He quickly grabbed a handful of apples while she snagged a flask of water, and together they joined the others at the table where they'd sat the night before.

Cosette was sitting there as well. As far as humanly possible from Seth.

"Hey," Evie sat beside her, feeling instantly protective at the fragile look on her face, "I don't remember you leaving this morning. Is everything okay?"

She'd spoken quietly, but Seth was a shifter. His face immediately stilled as he stopped what he was doing, secretly hanging on every word.

The little princess paused a moment, then continued peeling a slice of fruit.

"I went for a walk. Wanted to clear my head."

Seth's dark eyes flickered across the table, but Ellanden sat down in between.

"You shouldn't drink so much," he said sagely. "You probably shouldn't be drinking at all."

Evie's eyes snapped shut.

How can the man be so perceptive one moment, and so completely oblivious the next?

"You're right," Cosette said quietly, staring at the table. "I shouldn't drink so much."

"Speaking of last night," Freya interrupted through a mouthful of fruit, "I talked to the coven and they don't have what we need. I guess we'll just keep looking someplace else."

Cosette let out a quiet sigh, while Evie glanced between them curiously.

"What are you talking about? What don't the witches have?"

"A seeing stone," the princess replied softly, glancing up at the sky. "My parents will be getting worried soon. I usually check in by now."

For a split second, Evie's heart lifted.

"Well...that would be perfect, wouldn't it?" The others turned to her. "I know it's nothing we planned, but if your father were to find us—"

"You were sleeping for a long time," Cosette interrupted smoothly. "There are things out there that could do serious harm, even to a dragon."

Evie scoffed as an image of her fearless uncle flashed through her mind.

"But that wouldn't stop your dad—"

"No, it wouldn't," Cosette said pointedly as the implication hit home. "He would come looking for me anyway. And he could be killed for it. All because I lost the stone..."

Suddenly, the princess' recent behavior made sense. The way she'd pushed for them to move forward, even at their own risk. The way she'd grown quieter and quieter, glancing up at the sky.

Ellanden slipped his arm around her. "We'll find another stone."

Her shoulders slumped miserably. "How? I've checked every place we've gone and haven't seen one." She gestured blindly around the clearing. "There are three dozen witches here and none of them—"

"We'll fine another stone," he repeated, smoothing her hair. "As of a few weeks ago, it's our entire job description. We travel around professionally, looking for stones."

She smiled weakly at the joke, while Freya corrected him under her breath.

"As of a few *years* ago..."

"Besides," Ellanden continued, not hearing her, "a seeing stone is only good for a handful of uses anyway. Kailas and Serafina know that. If you don't check in right away, they won't necessarily assume the worst..."

He trailed off at the look on her face. It was the same expression mirrored in Seth and Freya, the one that reminded him once again. It was years, not weeks.

"Like I said," Cosette murmured, "you'd been asleep for a long time."

And awkward silence fell over the table, broken when Seth cleared his throat.

"Why don't you ask the chief about it?" he offered diplomatically, speaking to no one in particular. "The man's going to have a better idea of what resources are around here than we do."

Evie nodded in agreement, nibbling on the edge of an apple.

"Actually, that's not the only thing I wanted to talk with him about." She turned eagerly to Ellanden. "Did Eli tell you what I asked him? About the shipwreck?"

The fae pursed his lips. "We didn't really get that far."

Her eyes narrowed sarcastically. "Because you tortured him?"

Ellanden bypassed the water, pouring himself some ale. "Torture is such a strong word. If he ever wakes up, I'm sure he'll agree."

Seth glanced between them with a hint of alarm. "Wait...who did what?" His eyebrows lifted ever so slightly as he gestured back to the trees. "Was there a torture schedule this morning I wasn't made aware of?"

Evie rolled her eyes, waving it off dismissively. "It was just Eli. And trust me, he had it coming."

"Why?" Freya interjected. "Just because he was boasting last night?"

Ellanden glanced at Seth, casually twirling his knife. "I'd do it for less of a reason..."

"I'm serious," Freya insisted, wide-eyed with astonishment. "Just because he was boasting?"

Evie and the prince shared a quick glance. A silent request passed between them.

"Yes," he answered calmly. "Because he was boasting."

Evie glanced at him again before dropping her eyes to the table.

Thank you.

Seth shook his head slowly, staring across the table at the fae. "You are severely unhinged..."

Ellanden flashed a sweet smile, still holding the knife. "Careful now."

"I was actually surprised by what Eli said," Freya interrupted suddenly, leaning in between them. "I thought only your bloodline could shape-shift. Isn't that the Oberon legacy?"

Ellanden stiffened instinctively, eyes flickering around the camp.

"We're one of the few families. Eli was right about one thing: it's a rare gift."

Gift.

Funny he should choose that word. Evie didn't think she'd ever heard him call it that.

Yet sitting there in the clearing, it seemed impossible to deny it. By definition the Kreo were a diverse people, united by only one thing...magic.

It was everywhere. In the air, in the trees. The ground itself was soaking in it. Traces were flickering in the fire. The only reason the friends had been rescued was because a group had gone to the beach to pick fruit and practice their spells by the water. The princess was willing to bet that magic had brought them to the sandy shores as well. How else could they have survived the shipwreck? How else could they have been nursed back to health so quickly?

"I really need to speak with the chief," she murmured, almost to herself.

She wasn't quite sure from what bloodline the man hailed, but he was an embodiment of all the supernatural wonder around them. If anyone could give her answers, it would surely be him.

Cosette lifted her eyes, gesturing behind the table.

"Ask and you shall receive..."

Two men were walking side by side through the tall grass. One was old and squat and the very person she'd been looking for. The other had broken her heart just a few hours before.

This is why people shouldn't go on quests, she thought suddenly. *Because if you break up with someone halfway through, you have to stick around and see them day after day.*

A breath caught in her throat and she felt Ellanden's hand below the table—squeezing her knee reassuringly. His voice whispered into her ear a moment later, so quiet that even the shifters and the vampire would be unable to hear.

"I'm not taking sides...but do you want me to kick his arse?"

Never in her life had she been more grateful for the fae than she was in that moment. Her pulse evened and her face warmed with the hint of a secret smile.

The next second, the men were upon them.

"Hey," Asher greeted them briefly, his eyes flashing to the princess before lowering with a blush, "I was speaking with Rone this morning and he showed me a map."

In the blink of an eye, he produced a roll of parchment from the fold of his cloak. Despite the heat the vampire was still wearing one, almost like a shield between him and the outside world.

He spread it quickly on the table, pushing aside the apples and ale. "We're here."

The friends stood up at the same time, leaning over the table. They stared at his finger for a moment before making the long journey to the far side of the map.

"How is that possible?" Ellanden breathed. "We were five hundred leagues away..."

Rone's eyes twinkled as they swept the fae up and down.

"Storms have a way of doing that." He continued cryptically, "They also have a way of bringing us exactly where we need to be."

The princess was transfixed. The fae rolled his eyes.

"So how are we going to get back?" he said sharply, less impressed by the mystery of it than he was highly inconvenienced by it. "Because

I highly doubt we'd be able to waltz back through the Carpathian settlement and steal another ship."

There was a beat of silence.

"...not that we stole a ship."

The chief let out a burst of laughter that turned into a raspy cough halfway through. He took the prince's ale to steady himself, draining the glass in a single gulp.

"So *impatient*," he chided. "Did someone never stop and thank his lucky stars that he washed ashore in the first place? Your bones could be drifting to the bottom of the sea."

Ellanden smiled sweetly, grabbing himself another glass. "I'm not that lucky. The fates saw fit to bring me here instead."

Evie sucked in a silent breath, astonished by his lack of manners, but the chief took it all in stride. Even more than that, he seemed to be expecting it.

"Patience is a virtue, my child." His eyes twinkled at the look of silent rebellion on the fae's face. "Better you learn that lesson now, while there is still time, than have it be forced upon you in some darker story. The winds of providence can only—"

"—can only guide where you allow them to go," the fae finished crossly. "Yes, I'm well aware of the proverb." He jammed a finger down on the parchment. "Now can you offer us some guidance to make sense of these scribbles? Or shall we simply set off on our own?"

Evie's mouth fell open. Asher stared between them in shock.

"Ellanden," he scolded under his breath, "what are you—"

"No reason to lower your voice," the fae interrupted loudly, those eternal eyes fixed with a stab of annoyance on the old man. "Rone here knows *exactly* who I am. He knows who we all are."

The friends turned to the chief in amazement, only to be rewarded with a toothy grin.

"You'll forgive me if I don't curtsey...I've quite forgotten how."

Chapter 13

"But how did you *know*?" the princess asked for the hundredth time.

The rest of the villagers had wandered away from the clearing, going about their daily chores. But the friends were still sitting at the table, rooted in astonishment to the same spot.

"That proverb," Ellanden answered irritably, his eyes still on the chief, "is an old Kreo saying; one my mother taught me when I was a child. A rather cryptic introduction—"

Rone burst out laughing.

"As opposed to no introduction at all?" He took a step closer, looking the young fae up and down. "Our prince returns after ten years, a complete mystery as to where he was. He says not a word to reveal his identity, just seems content simply to drink our whiskey and go on his way." His eyes twinkled with another smile. "And you expect me not to have a little fun?"

A hard silence fell between them, broken by an unexpected voice.

"Your prince returns…in the back of a feed cart," Seth corrected casually. The others turned to him incredulously and he lifted a shoulder with a grin. "I feel it's important to make sure these stories are accurately recorded…for posterity's sake."

Ellanden ignored him, focused only on the chief. "So are you going to ask me?"

He said the words quietly, but there was a strange edge to his voice. A hint of defiance that was mirrored in his eyes. The chief stared at him a moment, then shook his head.

"I don't imagine that story is meant for me." His face grew unexpectedly thoughtful. "Least of all before your parents have heard it themselves. I'm assuming that you have not yet reached them," he continued, a bit sharper. "Otherwise I doubt we would have met in such a manner."

Evie took a sudden step forward, speaking in spite of herself.

"Do you think you could get a message to them?" she pleaded. "If it was even just to tell them that we're alive—"

The chief nodded slowly, lost in thought. "There might be a way. In the morning, some of my people were to set sail for the next village. We generally keep to ourselves—it's safer that way—but we occasionally need to leave our borders in order to gather supplies. There's a woman who lives there, an old woman, who might be able to help." He nodded at Ellanden. "If your mother is still with the rest of them, the two of us might be able to make a connection—send a message she'd be able to hear."

The fae froze perfectly still, unable to believe such a thing might come to pass.

"Tomorrow," he repeated shakily. "I could speak with her…tomorrow."

Rone's eyes warmed with a gentle smile. "It takes time to sail. Not to mention that I have no idea whether the witch in question is even alive. But…yes. There's a chance you could speak to your mother in the next few days."

Ellanden took a step back. A kind of shiver swept over him. Suddenly, he found himself feeling what the others had been saying all along. It had been years, not weeks. Ten impossible years.

He couldn't bring himself to speak. He simply nodded, eyes on the ground.

"If that's the plan, then I suppose preparations are in order." The chief clapped his hands briskly, taking a moment to straighten the dead bat atop his head. "I suggest you all take the day to rest, gather your strength. Pack what you have, and I'll see you all at dinner."

The friends nodded in swift agreement, pushing to their feet. The old man was already halfway across the meadow by the time the princess caught up with him.

"Rone!" she called out before catching herself quickly. "I mean...Chief?"

He turned around with a chuckle, deepening the creases around his eyes. "If that impetuous young fae truly is the High Priest of the Kreo, then I can only imagine who you might be. I can scarcely remember hearing a story from the High Kingdom without the both of you in it together."

She blushed immediately, cringing at what stories he might have heard. "You've done so much for us already, I'm sorry to ask for something more." Her eyes lifted slowly, staring back at him. "But I was wondering—"

"You were wondering about the shipwreck," he answered plainly.

Her mouth fell open in astonishment.

"How did you..."

For such a squat old man, he drew himself up to an impressive height.

"My dear, you are looking at one of the last chiefs of the Kreo. A people bound by magic and blessed with such power so as to challenge the heavens and lay waste to the minds of men."

She blinked.

"...Eli told me."

Oh, that makes sense.

"You'll probably think it doesn't matter," she said quietly. "The ship sank, what's done is done. But there are things I need to remember. Answers I need."

The chief stared at her in silence. She could have sworn the bat fluttered a wing. Then he leaned towards her with a conspiratorial smile.

"My dear...you would have made a fine Kreo yourself."

She let out a breath, brightening with a smile.

"So you'll help me?" she asked eagerly. "I heard there were things you could do to help restore one's memory. My Aunt Tanya said there were spells and potions—"

He held up a hand, nodding all the while. "Yes, we have ways of unlocking the mind. Come to my cabin at sundown—we'll work it out then." He raised his voice, glancing back to where Ellanden was pretending not to watch them from the corner of his eye. "You're welcome to come as well, Your Highness."

Ellanden's spine stiffened as he turned away. "I'm fine without your voodoo spells, thanks."

Rone walked away with a chuckle, leaving the friends behind. "You might learn something..."

THE REST OF THE DAY passed with excruciating slowness, each hour dragging on longer than the last. Not one of the friends was immune, and by the time the sun finally began to slip towards the jungle tempers were running at an all-time high.

Freya was sad to be leaving the witches, Seth and Cosette were giving each other a wide berth. Evie and Asher were both doing their best not to look at each other, and Ellanden was sitting between them—staring in silence at a pair of young warlocks practicing magic on the lawn.

They had been going at it for almost an hour, the palms of their hands glowing every so often as they recited a chant or spell. It went on in quiet repetition, until all at once a shimmer of light passed between them triumphantly. Ellanden leaned back, a strange expression on his face.

Asher gave him a nudge. "You want to go join them?"

The fae shot him a look, but kept silent. He had been doing his best to scorn the vampire on Evie's behalf, but when it became clear that she had no intention of holding a grudge he began to tire of the notion himself. At any rate, there were other things on his mind.

"You're not just Fae," Asher coaxed quietly. "You're also Kreo."

The prince shifted uncomfortably, gazing out at his unwitting subjects. It wasn't simply that he didn't like to talk about it, he just didn't seem to know what to make of it himself. It was a pairing of contradictions. The cool refinement of the Fae, and the fiery chaos of his mother's tribe. When he was just a young child, he'd chosen a side. But it was impossible to fully repress the other.

"They're not even a people," he muttered. "They're just…a mix of everything."

"Like you," Asher said gently.

"Really?" the fae shot back. "*You* want to get into that? The merits of cultural pride?"

The vampire dropped his gaze, giving the sword he was holding another twirl.

Earlier that morning, as he was wandering despondently away from the princess, Rone had summoned him unexpectedly and sat down for a chat. He'd apologized again for the attack on the beach, but tried to put it into perspective. The Kreo had been terrorized by vampires for the better part of a decade. It was one of the reasons the camp was hidden—they'd learned to kill them on sight.

It was a guilt that Asher felt heavily, but it was secretly matched by Ellanden.

Staring around the little camp, it was impossible to deny that each person was united by something more than just magic…they were refugees.

When the three friends had run away from the royal caravan, they'd set into motion a series of events that the fates themselves couldn't have predicted. A decade-long search, a decade-long decline. A decade without the leadership and protection necessary to hold the realm together.

These people had needed a prince. And now he was leaving again.

"We can come back," Cosette murmured, reading his thoughts. "Of all the people who will benefit from what we're trying to do—these have the most to gain. Once we've completed our mission, you can come back and tell them what happened in person."

"Who knows," Seth added cheerfully, "you might even want to stay." Ellanden lifted his eyes slowly and he flashed a friendly smile. "You'd look great in one of those bat-crowns."

The rest of the day passed in similar fashion. Trying to ignore each other, trying to remember what had happened, trying not to think of everything yet to come.

There were many steps to get through first, but the one thing the friends weren't talking about was the ship. Not the one they'd sunk. The one they now needed.

As it stood, warships were in short supply. They could try to barter passage on a merchant vessel, but they'd have a hard time trying to convince a captain to take them towards the Dunes. As if the destination wasn't enough, there was the voyage itself. Everything they'd acquired had been lost when the ship vanished into the sea. Their weapons, their clothes, their coin...

They were gearing up for a dangerous adventure without anything more than the clothes on their backs. The most they could expect from the village was a generous supply of henna.

"Is it that time again?" Cosette said suddenly, lifting her head in surprise.

The grassy clearing, which had been deserted for the better part of the day, was suddenly awash with activity. People were flooding in from all corners, setting up for the nightly feast.

Evie's eyes strayed to a pair of half-dressed shifters as they began to light the fire. If she'd thought the village was putting on a show in honor of their arrival, she was clearly mistaken. The Kreo put on a spectacle every day of the week.

Even Seth, who'd grown up in a pack of shifters and was effectively immune to nudity, found himself struck speechless—lowering his eyes quickly when a pair of witches sashayed past.

"You're right," Ellanden said suddenly as a lovely nymph flashed a seductive smile. "This place looks fine to me." He headed off without a backwards glance. "See you guys at dinner."

The rest of them stared after him in surprise as he met the woman across the clearing. They spoke for only a moment before she laced her fingers through his, leading him off into the trees.

"Unbelievable," Cosette muttered, shaking her head.

"Can you blame him?" Asher grinned, recycling Freya's favorite joke. "It's been ten years."

But for once the witch wasn't laughing.

"That's not funny," she snapped, pushing to her feet.

Cosette followed immediately after her, throwing the vampire a punishing look over her shoulder. Seth pushed to his feet as well, casting a final glance at Ellanden.

"I'd find that shape-shifter first...just to be sure."

Evie laughed under her breath, then froze in a sudden panic when she realized who the only other person left sitting at the table was. Asher realized it at the same time as she did herself, tensing automatically before throwing her a quick glance from the corner of his eye.

Thus far, they'd done a magnificent job of avoiding one another—especially considering they'd been sitting less than ten feet away. With a table of friends to separate them, a village of people to distract them, and an apocalyptic prophecy to motivate them, it had been possible to compartmentalize their break-up as a problem for another day. Not easy, but possible.

Now...there wasn't a chance.

"Can we talk?"

Evie jumped in surprise, glancing over at him.

Well that's a terrible way to start.

"Uh...I should actually..." She trailed off, wracking her brain for something to say. "I should probably get to the..."

I'm stranded in the middle of the jungle. Where exactly am I supposed to go?

Asher stared at her a moment, then his shoulders bowed in a quiet sigh. "Evie...please. Can we talk?"

This time, she held his gaze—biting her lip almost angrily as they stared across the table. It went on for a few moments then she pushed abruptly to her feet, heading swiftly into the jungle.

He pushed tentatively to his feet, staring after her.

"...is that a yes?"

She cocked her head and he quickly followed her, vanishing into the trees.

THE PRINCESS AND THE vampire wandered around for a while, both unsure where they wanted to end up. Her room was most likely occupied by a scowling witch and a vengeful fae. But the last time they were in his room...things hadn't ended very well.

At last, they came to a sort of compromise, coming to a stop at a random viewpoint cut halfway up the abandoned tree. They glanced just once at the blazing sunset before averting their eyes. Asher cocked his head awkwardly at the bench, and they both took a seat.

At least it's treacherously high, she thought miserably. *If things start going wrong, I can just jump—*

"I want to apologize," Asher said quietly.

She whirled around to face him, but he kept his eyes on the trees.

"All day I've been replaying what happened," he admitted, "and it occurred to me that I phrased things in a way that made it seem like you were to blame."

Her lips parted, but she said nothing. He sounded oddly rehearsed.

"*I* was to blame," he concluded softly. "Every bit of fault lies with me."

The princess flinched like he'd struck her. Her eyes prickled with secret tears. "Would you stop—"

"No, Evie, it's important that you understand this." He finally turned towards her, gazing directly into her eyes. "This was *my* mistake—not yours. Thinking that something like this was possible, not recognizing the damage it would do from the start... You had no way of predicting such a thing, but I should have known better. If I could take it back, I swear that I would—"

"Would you *stop*!" she cried again, sliding away from him on the bench. "Are you not listening to yourself? Do you not realize the way this sounds?"

He stared back incredulously and she shook her head, wiping away furious tears.

"I was about to have *sex* with you, Asher. That might not register much with you, but it means a heck of a lot to me. It was going to be my *first* time. And I wanted it to be with *you*."

She sucked in a quick breath, almost unable to finish.

"And you wish you could take the whole thing *back*?"

He held up his hands quickly, closing his eyes.

"That's not what I meant. There's nothing that I..." He trailed off, trying to think of a way to phrase it. "Evie, you have *no idea* how much I wanted that, too, but—"

"But what?" she demanded. "But now it was just a mistake?"

"*But now it hurt you*!" he shouted, finally raising his voice. "A moment like that...and it *hurt* you, Everly. Not because of anything you did, but because of *me*. Because of what *I am*!"

"You didn't do anything wrong," she insisted, breathing so quickly she was beginning to feel light in the head. "I was...I was startled by the blood. But that doesn't mean—"

"It doesn't mean what?" He put his hands on her shoulders, staring at her straight on. "It doesn't mean that I'm some kind of monster? The one who attacked Ellanden, the same one who attacked you in that cave? I'll never be able to take back those moments, Evie. And then last night, the one time you needed to trust me the most..."

He looked away quickly, shivering as the last of the sunlight vanished in the trees.

"It was different when we were at the palace," he breathed. "I wasn't a vampire, you weren't a shifter, and Ellanden wasn't a fae. We were just kids. We were just people. But out here...?"

A look of physical pain flashed across his face.

"You cried when I reached for you. You pulled away from me on the bed. And you were *right* to do so. What those witches tried to do on the beach...they were right. There's a reason my people are reviled and feared. There's a reason we don't get to love people like you."

A ringing silence fell between them.

Then Evie's face whitened in shock.

In hindsight, she'd never understand the timing. She'd never know why it took him condemning himself to darkness in order for her to see the light.

But in the midst of all those shadows, the truth was suddenly clear to see.

He might have been born a vampire. She might have been born the daughter of a king. They might have been sailing off on some ill-fated adventure, and if the prophecy was right there was a good chance one of them wasn't coming back.

But none of that mattered.

Because she was in love with him.

"I love you, too."

He blinked quickly, then shook his head.

"...what?"

She pushed abruptly to her feet.

"We should get to the feast."

She was off a moment later, winding her way down the rickety rope-bridges that clung to the sides of the trees. He hesitated a split second, staring in a delayed kind of shock, then he rushed after her—blurring to her side with a rush of vampiric speed.

"I don't understand what just happened—"

"That must be frustrating."

"I thought you said we could talk—"

"We did."

He started to speak again, but she turned around suddenly—lifting a finger to his lips. He shivered the moment they touched, staring down at her with wide, dilated eyes.

"We did talk," she said again, staring up with a little smile. "And it was a good talk, Ash."

She continued walking a moment later, leaving him standing in complete bewilderment on the swaying steps. It wasn't the best timing for such a revelation—the moment their relationship had come to an abrupt end—but somehow, she wouldn't trade it for anything in the world. Because somehow, it was only the beginning. The vampire just didn't realize it yet.

That little smile stayed with her, lighting her face as she headed into the dark.

A really good talk...

THE PRINCESS GOT BACK to the clearing just as the feast was getting started. The musicians were tuning their fiddles, the fire was crackling, and scores of witches were heading out from beneath the jungle canopy—balancing platter after platter on their painted arms.

She lifted her arm when she caught sight of her friends, about to wave them over, when a cool hand closed suddenly over her wrist. She turned around to see Asher standing behind her.

That look of bewilderment hadn't gone away. It was getting worse by the second.

"What?" she asked, almost enjoying herself.

Since they were children, she and Ellanden had always loved those rare moments when the vampire floundered. Of the three of them, he was always so sure of himself. That quiet composure carried him from moment to moment. It was nearly impossible to catch him off guard.

Landi's going to be sad he missed this.

"I'm sorry, I just...what happened back there?" He stared down at her in a complete loss, even more confused by that inexplicable smile. "I was just trying to apologize—"

"I heard."

"I said people like us could never be together—"

"You did."

"And then you said...that you love me, too?"

She smiled again, immortalizing the priceless image in her mind. "You have summarized it perfectly."

He stared intently for a moment, then repeated his original statement. "I don't understand what's going on."

She let out a quiet breath, staring up into his eyes. "Ash, you can speech-make all you want. You can declare yourself unworthy, and call yourself a monster, and say the witches were really on to something special when they tried to drown you in the sea. But that doesn't change the fact that I fell in love with you."

He froze perfectly still, unable to think of a single reply.

"Like I said...it was a good talk."

She left without another word, joining the others at the edge of the clearing. One of their members was still missing, but judging by the look on Freya's face they'd just found him.

Seven hells.

The prince was glued at the mouth to the breathtaking nymph they'd seen before. One hand fiddling with the back of her silken gown, the other tangled in her long, wavy hair.

"*Ellanden*," she said loudly, startling him to attention.

He jerked back in surprise and the nymph let out a little shriek and promptly turned into a tree, shivering agitatedly in the breeze. His eyes snapped shut and he banged his head comically against its branches before turning around with a tight smile to greet his friends.

"What?"

"We're getting some food," the princess replied with a grin. "You want to come? Or were you and that tree going to do something special?"

The fae murmured what sounded like an apology before following his friends reluctantly into the clearing, throwing wistful glances over his shoulder every few steps. Asher joined them at the table, still looking like he'd seen a ghost. But no sooner had they sat down than the princess pushed straight back to her feet again, realizing all at once there was something she needed to do.

"I'm off to see Rone. Save me some ale, will you?"

Freya shook her head decisively, while Ellanden pushed to his feet.

"You're really doing that?" he asked skeptically. "He's really going to try to help you get back your memories?"

"Of course," she declared, like it was something that happened every day. "Why in the world wouldn't he?"

The fae stared at her a moment longer, weighing her determination, then grabbed a biscuit off the table and popped it into his mouth. "All right, I'm ready. Let's go."

The princess glanced up in surprise. "Really? You're coming?"

He adjusted his cloak, rolling his eyes at the same time. "Do you mean...am I letting you get drugged in a jungle hut by some old man? All by yourself? No, I am not."

Asher flashed him a silent look of gratitude as the two friends headed off into the night.

THE CHIEF'S HUT WAS at the far edge of the village—a place where the sounds of the feast had faded to a gentle hum. The friends spotted it from a ways off and slowly began walking towards it, hands in their pockets as they wandered beneath the stars.

"Are you nervous?" Ellanden finally asked.

Evie nodded silently, watching a trail of smoke drifting up from the hut. "You know...you were pretty hard on Rone this morning."

The fae rolled his eyes. "Rone's a lot tougher than I am. He can take it."

She glanced at him curiously. "Still, why—"

"It's just so typical of the way they do things," he interrupted, a hint of that old irritation seeping back into his voice. "Their prince returns home, and instead of saying anything he's given a necklace of bones and carried in with the mangos."

A group of warlocks went barreling past them, and he let out a sigh.

"This just isn't me. When I was younger, I tried. For my mother's sake. I'd go with her every summer. I'd try to give it a chance, but...it isn't me."

Evie remembered the first few times Ellanden had returned from the hot Kreo desert, back into the cool embrace of his beloved Taviel. She remembered how Leonor, the head of his father's council, had been delighted in the prince's discomfort. Stoking those flames every chance he could.

One year in particular, the prince had come back painted head to toe in swirls of amber henna. He didn't say anything. He simply looked at his father, then headed to his room.

The summer after, he was no longer forced to return.

Still, she refused to think that all the memories were bad. She'd seen the look on his face when they'd first set foot in the camp. The way he'd smelled the flowers, the way he'd repeated their collective chant, a little smile creeping up his face.

Then there was the way he'd been watching the warlocks.

"You never wonder what it would be like?" she asked. "To be able to do all those incredible things yourself?"

It wasn't just the shape-shifting. His mother could whip up potions and elixirs just as easily as any witch. His grandmother could open portals to a different place in time. At one point in their childhood both women had spontaneously sprouted angel wings, taking to the sky.

Ellanden paused a moment, then shook his head.

"No," he lied. "I never wonder what it's like."

She snorted sarcastically. "Sure. And I never wonder what it would be like to be a dragon..."

When they reached the tent, two things became immediately clear. First, that was not ordinary smoke rising from the chimney. And second, there was no way to knock.

"This is what I mean," Ellanden muttered, pulling back the animal-skin flap with a rather disgusted look on his face. "All this power, yet they live like savages—"

"The savages can hear you," a voice answered from inside.

The princess shot him a smug look, and together they ducked inside.

In hindsight, the chief's hut was nothing like what she thought it would be. She'd expected a reflection of the man himself, but the place couldn't have been more different. The walls were clean and sparse, the floor was neatly swept. There was a bed in the corner, along with a few simple pieces of furniture, but other than that the place was nearly empty.

Except for the dead snake in the middle of the floor.

"Seven hells!" Evie let out a gasp without thinking, grabbing the fae. "What is that doing here? Is it really dead? Landi—poke it to be sure!"

The words all ran together as the chief pulled himself away from the fire he was tending in the corner, straightening up to greet them with a twinkling smile.

"It's undoubtedly deceased," he assured her. "I drowned the thing myself."

For whatever reason, that didn't help soothe her nerves. She eyed it warily, still angled defensively behind the fae, when Ellanden swept forward and put it on the table.

She stared at him in baffled silence.

First that he would touch it. Then that he hadn't thrown it outside.

Maybe he was right to avoid this place. It's a bad influence.

"So that's what it is?" he asked in an oddly practiced voice. "The venom?"

She stared a second longer, then her eyes widened in illumination.

All her life, she'd assumed the Oberon women had made their little brews from flowers, or herbs, or other palatable ingredients. Never would she have imagined it was something like this.

Rone nodded routinely, gesturing for them to sit on the floor.

"Vials are on the table. You're welcome to do the honors."

Unaware that the princess' eyes were following his every move Ellanden picked up a glass tube and the snake before settling down beside her, handling both as if it was the most casual thing in the world. With a look of intense concentration he lifted one to the other, pressing the fangs ever so carefully to the lid of the jar. A thin stream of liquid poured forth, trickling down the sides.

"Just a touch," Rone instructed, watching over his shoulder. "More than that and she won't be able to come back."

Ellanden hesitated a moment, then handed both things to the chief.

"You do it," he said stiffly. "I don't want to make a mistake."

"That's the only way we learn—"

"He can learn on someone else," Evie interrupted with alarm. "You do it."

The chief chuckled quietly, lifting the vial as he sprayed in tiny drops of venom from the teeth of the snake. Ellanden's eyes followed every move, watching closely. The princess sucked in a quick breath, trying to brace herself for what was about to come.

She didn't know what she was hoping to find. She wasn't entirely sure why'd she had asked the chief in the first place. The others couldn't remember the shipwreck either. But all of them had laid those burning questions to rest. Why was it that she alone was plagued with the mystery? Unable to chalk it up to providence like the rest of them and simply let it go.

Because it's not just about the shipwreck. It's also about my dreams—

"Are you ready?"

She lifted her eyes to see Rone sitting right in front of her, offering the glass vial. She took it then, turning it over with profound hesitation, glancing instinctively at Ellanden by her side.

"I'll be right here," he said softly.

She nodded quickly, taking his hand.

Sitting on the floor, holding a vial full of venom, she suddenly realized the real reason he'd offered to come with her. She loved him for it even more.

"Drink quickly and try not to resist," Rone advised. "In order for your vision to expand, you must open yourself to it. Release all expectations and allow yourself to be carried along."

The princess nodded, staring into the vial.

Try not to resist. Right.

Before she could talk herself out of it, she downed the venom like a shot—setting the vial down quickly and bracing herself against the floor, ready for whatever was coming next.

For a few seconds, nothing happened. She heard the crackling of the fire. She felt the warmth of Ellanden's hand. Then all at once, the princess crumpled noiselessly to the floor...

※

IT WAS LIKE TRYING to remember a dream, even as it was happening. Blending time and reality as a story you'd always carried inside you, played out before your eyes...

Evie stared around in a daze, trying to get her bearings as the ground beneath her quaked and writhed. Gone was the fire, gone was the hut. The land itself had vanished, and she was sailing on the open seas. A second later, she saw the lightning. A second later, she heard the screams.

It was one thing being lost in the chaos of the moment. It was another thing entirely to see that moment play out in perfect clarity before your eyes. The princess watched as she and her friends were thrown violently from one side of the ship to another, pitched back and forth as it rocked from side to side. Looking at it from a distance, it was a miracle they'd managed to say on board so long. With each wave, she thought they were done for. Each time water streamed over the railing, she had no idea why it didn't sweep them straight out into the churning maelstrom.

Of course, there were several details that she'd missed.

Twice, Asher released his death-grip on the banister to go diving after her—pulling her back to safety just before she could slip into the waves. Three times. Then four. There seemed no limit to the number of times he would risk his life, no limit to the things he would do to just to keep her alive. It was no wonder she couldn't remember. She would highly doubt the vampire remembered himself. But as the world fell apart around them, they clung to each other in the middle of the ship, illuminated by flashes of lightning as they braced themselves against the storm.

But such a thing was never meant to last.

When the boat began cracking up the middle, each friend went white with fear. The noise alone was terrifying, coming from deep within the ship itself. Splintered boards went flying skyward, hurtling through the air.

Cosette was screaming something, but no one could hear her. The rest of them were scrambling farther up the deck, but none of them would make it in time. In what looked like slow motion, the two halves of the vessel split apart—throwing everyone still clinging to its broken pieces out into the churning waves.

It didn't take long to realize the storm was too powerful. They wouldn't be able to swim. One by one their heads vanished into the shadowy water, disappearing without a trace.

Evie held her breath, diving down with them.

It was utterly bizarre—to view such a thing from within the calming lens of sleep. She watched with perfect clarity as they were thrashed beneath the waves just as fiercely as they'd been above, helpless playthings of a vengeful storm.

Seth was struck over the back of the head with a fragment of the ship's keel. His arms floated up in front of him as his eyes fluttered closed. Cosette was kicking towards the surface with all her might, but the pull of the ship continued dragging her down, too strong for even a princess of the Fae to withstand. Asher tried to grab her as she flashed by, but he was quickly struck with debris and drifted lifelessly down beside her, still reaching out his hand.

There were only two people still moving—both in the greatest trouble of all.

Ellanden was awake and kicking but he was tangled in one of the riggings, the thick rope digging into his sides. He harder he fought the greater it ensnared him, dragging him farther and farther down into the sea.

Even knowing the outcome, that he was currently safe and dry and sitting beside her, it was still hard to watch. There didn't seem to be any hope for him...until a beautiful girl appeared by his side.

STRENGTH

How Freya was able to reach him, the princess would never know. All she remembered was her look of fierce determination as she lifted her hands to the rigging, blasting the rope loose. Again and again bursts of light shot from her palms, but they were running out of time.

She kicked to the surface, kissing a burst of life-saving air into his mouth. For a split second the world steadied, but as she kicked off to do it again he realized it was helpless. He was sinking too far down. Instead he caught her wrist, shaking his head and pointing her up toward the surface for good. A last desperate bid for freedom, saving one life instead of losing two before they were swallowed forever by the darkness, never to be seen again.

But she refused to part with him. She refused to leave his side. As lightning flashed above, illuminating the sea around them, she laced her fingers through his, holding on for all she was worth as the two silently vanished into the sea.

Evie blinked after them in horror, having already lost sight of all the rest.

It would have been impossible to save them, let alone move them, let alone FIND them. All of them had vanished, their lives claimed by a raging and violent sea.

'So what happened?' she thought desperately. 'What could have possibly...?'

All at once, she went still—listening as a chorus of voices echoed softly beneath the waves. At first she thought she was just imagining it, but louder and louder it grew, overwhelming her with the certainty of one thing.

They were not alone.

There was a great shadow moving in the distance, too far away to make out a shape. She tried swimming towards it, squinting her eyes against the water only to see other eyes staring back at her. They were beautiful, faceless, a thousand different colors glinting in the depths of the ocean despite there being no sun.

She stared in fascination, listening as those sing-song voices drifted along the waves.

An overwhelming impulse swept over her. She had to get closer. She had to find out what those singing voices meant. The fate of the world depended on it. The lives of her friends. If only she could get closer—

Then all at once, a cold current swept out of nowhere—lifting her with the tide.

The eyes vanished. Those singing voices faded into the depths as she and the others were taken somewhere far away, out of the ocean's grasp—

Evie opened her eyes with a gasp, panting for air as if she was still underwater.

No longer was she in the ocean, but back in the chief's hut. The colors steadied and the dizziness vanished, but there was something wrong here as well.

It wasn't cold, as she remembered. It was hot. Too hot.

Her eyes lifted slowly, dazzled by the flames.

The hut was on fire.

"Ellanden?" she gasped, unable to pull her eyes away.

There were screams coming from outside, echoing across the length of the camp. Through the open flap, she saw people running as if their lives depended upon it—chased by what looked like shadows of liquid smoke. She watched with wide eyes as one caught up with a warlock, ripping back his head before showering the ground with a splash of blood. The body fell with a thud very near to the entrance of the dwelling. She pulled back in horror, understanding for the first time why everyone was screaming. What those shadows really were.

Her blood ran cold and her face paled with fright.

Vampires.

THE END

VALIDATION – Book 6 blurb

THE WORLD KEEPS TURNING... so be careful not to fall out of step.

When the Kreo settlement falls under attack, Evie and her friends are spirited away to the last place in the world they'd ever want to be...a vampire prison. With the fate of the kingdoms hanging in the balance they bind themselves to an unlikely ally, sealing a covenant they might give their lives to keep.

The prophecy is waiting. A silent adversary is moving in the dark.

Can the friends recover the lost stone?

Can they find the missing pieces and restore balance to the realm?

Or will they be forced to ask the fateful question?

...are they already too late?

The Queen's Alpha Series

Eternal
Everlasting
Unceasing
Evermore
Forever
Boundless
Prophecy
Protected
Foretelling
Revelation
Betrayal
Resolved

The Omega Queen Series

Discipline
Bravery
Courage
Conquer
Strength
Validation
Approval
Blessing
Balance
Grievance
Enchanted
Gratified

Find W.J. May

Website:
http://www.wjmaybooks.com
Facebook:
https://www.facebook.com/pages/Author-WJ-May-FAN-PAGE/141170442608149
Newsletter:
SIGN UP FOR W.J. May's Newsletter to find out about new releases, updates, cover reveals and even freebies!
http://eepurl.com/97aYf

More books by W.J. May

The Chronicles of Kerrigan

BOOK I - *Rae of Hope* is **FREE!**
Book Trailer:
http://www.youtube.com/watch?v=gILAwXxx8MU
Book II - *Dark Nebula*
Book Trailer:
http://www.youtube.com/watch?v=Ca24STi_bFM
Book III - *House of Cards*
Book IV - *Royal Tea*
Book V - *Under Fire*
Book VI - *End in Sight*
Book VII – *Hidden Darkness*
Book VIII – *Twisted Together*
Book IX – *Mark of Fate*
Book X – *Strength & Power*
Book XI – *Last One Standing*
BOOK XII – *Rae of Light*

PREQUEL –
Christmas Before the Magic
Question the Darkness
Into the Darkness
Fight the Darkness
Alone the Darkness
Lost the Darkness

SEQUEL –
    Matter of Time
    Time Piece
    Second Chance
    Glitch in Time
    Our Time
    Precious Time

Hidden Secrets Saga:
Download Seventh Mark part 1 For FREE
Book Trailer:
http://www.youtube.com/watch?v=Y-_vVYC1gvo

Like most teenagers, Rouge is trying to figure out who she is and what she wants to be. With little knowledge about her past, she has questions but has never tried to find the answers. Everything changes when she befriends a strangely intoxicating family. Siblings Grace and Michael, appear to have secrets which seem connected to Rouge. Her hunch is confirmed when a horrible incident occurs at an outdoor party. Rouge may be the only one who can find the answer.

An ancient journal, a Sioghra necklace and a special mark force life-altering decisions for a girl who grew up unprepared to fight for her life or others.

All secrets have a cost and Rouge's determination to find the truth can only lead to trouble...or something even more sinister.

RADIUM HALOS - THE SENSELESS SERIES
Book 1 is FREE

Everyone needs to be a hero at one point in their life.

The small town of Elliot Lake will never be the same again.

Caught in a sudden thunderstorm, Zoe, a high school senior from Elliot Lake, and five of her friends take shelter in an abandoned uranium mine. Over the next few days, Zoe's hearing sharpens drastically, beyond what any normal human being can detect. She tells her friends, only to learn that four others have an increased sense as well. Only Kieran, the new boy from Scotland, isn't affected.

Fashioning themselves into superheroes, the group tries to stop the strange occurrences happening in their little town. Muggings, break-ins, disappearances, and murder begin to hit too close to home. It leads the team to think someone knows about their secret - someone who wants them all dead.

An incredulous group of heroes. A traitor in the midst. Some dreams are written in blood.

Courage Runs Red
The Blood Red Series
Book 1 is FREE

WHAT IF COURAGE WAS your only option?

When Kallie lands a college interview with the city's new hot-shot police officer, she has no idea everything in her life is about to change. The detective is young, handsome and seems to have an unnatural ability to stop the increasing local crime rate. Detective Liam's particular interest in Kallie sends her heart and head stumbling over each other.

When a raging blood feud between vampires spills into her home, Kallie gets caught in the middle. Torn between love and family loyalty she must find the courage to fight what she fears the most and possibly risk everything, even if it means dying for those she loves.

Daughter of Darkness - Victoria
Only Death Could Stop Her Now
The Daughters of Darkness is a series of female heroines who may or may not know each other, but all have the same father, Vlad Montour. Victoria is a Hunter Vampire

HUNTRESS SERIES
USA TODAY BESTSELLING AUTHOR
W.J. MAY
LOOK BACK
MASTER
PERMISSION

PROPHECY SERIES
USA TODAY BESTSELLING AUTHOR
• W.J. MAY •
PROPHECY
PROPHECY
PROPHECY

STRENGTH

Don't miss out!

Visit the website below and you can sign up to receive emails whenever W.J. May publishes a new book. There's no charge and no obligation.

https://books2read.com/r/B-A-SSF-UOTFB

BOOKS 2 READ

Connecting independent readers to independent writers.

Also by W.J. May

Bit-Lit Series
Lost Vampire
Cost of Blood
Price of Death

Blood Red Series
Courage Runs Red
The Night Watch
Marked by Courage
Forever Night
The Other Side of Fear
Blood Red Box Set Books #1-5

Daughters of Darkness: Victoria's Journey
Victoria
Huntress
Coveted (A Vampire & Paranormal Romance)
Twisted
Daughter of Darkness - Victoria - Box Set

Great Temptation Series
The Devil's Footsteps
Heaven's Command
Mortals Surrender

Hidden Secrets Saga
Seventh Mark - Part 1
Seventh Mark - Part 2
Marked By Destiny
Compelled
Fate's Intervention
Chosen Three
The Hidden Secrets Saga: The Complete Series

Kerrigan Chronicles
Stopping Time
A Passage of Time
Ticking Clock
Secrets in Time
Time in the City
Ultimate Future

Mending Magic Series
Lost Souls
Illusion of Power
Challenging the Dark

Castle of Power
Limits of Magic
Protectors of Light

Omega Queen Series
Discipline
Bravery
Courage
Conquer
Strength
Validation

Paranormal Huntress Series
Never Look Back
Coven Master
Alpha's Permission
Blood Bonding
Oracle of Nightmares
Shadows in the Night
Paranormal Huntress BOX SET

Prophecy Series
Only the Beginning
White Winter
Secrets of Destiny

Royal Factions
The Price For Peace
The Cost for Surviving

The Chronicles of Kerrigan
Rae of Hope
Dark Nebula
House of Cards
Royal Tea
Under Fire
End in Sight
Hidden Darkness
Twisted Together
Mark of Fate
Strength & Power
Last One Standing
Rae of Light
The Chronicles of Kerrigan Box Set Books # 1 - 6

The Chronicles of Kerrigan: Gabriel
Living in the Past
Present For Today
Staring at the Future

The Chronicles of Kerrigan Prequel
Christmas Before the Magic

Question the Darkness
Into the Darkness
Fight the Darkness
Alone in the Darkness
Lost in Darkness
The Chronicles of Kerrigan Prequel Series Books #1-3

The Chronicles of Kerrigan Sequel
A Matter of Time
Time Piece
Second Chance
Glitch in Time
Our Time
Precious Time

The Hidden Secrets Saga
Seventh Mark (part 1 & 2)

The Kerrigan Kids
School of Potential
Myths & Magic
Kith & Kin
Playing With Power
Line of Ancestry
Descent of Hope

The Queen's Alpha Series
Eternal
Everlasting
Unceasing
Evermore
Forever
Boundless
Prophecy
Protected
Foretelling
Revelation
Betrayal
Resolved
The Queen's Alpha Box Set

The Senseless Series
Radium Halos - Part 1
Radium Halos - Part 2
Nonsense
Perception
The Senseless - Box Set Books #1-4

Standalone
Shadow of Doubt (Part 1 & 2)
Five Shades of Fantasy
Zwarte Nevel
Shadow of Doubt - Part 1
Shadow of Doubt - Part 2

Four and a Half Shades of Fantasy
Dream Fighter
What Creeps in the Night
Forest of the Forbidden
Arcane Forest: A Fantasy Anthology
The First Fantasy Box Set

Watch for more at www.wjmaybooks.com.

About the Author

About W.J. May

Welcome to USA TODAY BESTSELLING author W.J. May's Page! SIGN UP for W.J. May's Newsletter to find out about new releases, updates, cover reveals and even freebies! http://eepurl.com/97aYf

Website: http://www.wjmaybooks.com

Facebook: http://www.facebook.com/pages/Author-WJ-May-FAN-PAGE/141170442608149?ref=hl *Please feel free to connect with me and share your comments. I love connecting with my readers.*

W.J. May grew up in the fruit belt of Ontario. Crazy-happy childhood, she always has had a vivid imagination and loads of energy. After her father passed away in 2008, from a six-year battle with cancer (which she still believes he won the fight against), she began to write again. A passion she'd loved for years, but realized life was too short to keep putting it off. She is a writer of Young Adult, Fantasy Fiction and where ever else her little muses take her.

Read more at www.wjmaybooks.com.

Printed in Great Britain
by Amazon